Secret Things
Twelve Tales to Terrify

STACEY LONGO

Books & Boos Press
PO Box 772
Hebron, CT 06248
booksandboospress.com

"Good Night, Francine" first published in *Malicious Deviance*
© 2011 Library of Horror Press
"Cliffhanger" first published in *Anthology: Year One*
© 2012 Four Horsemen Press
"Love Stinks" first published in *Hell Hath No Fury*
© 2012 May December Publications
"People Person" first published in *Dark Things IV: A Horror Anthology* ©
2010 Pill Hill Press
"Mother's Day" first published as "Zombie Mama" in *ZombiDays:
Festivities of the Flesheaters*
© 2011 Library of Horror Press
"Nobody Ever Listens to Eddie" first published in *Insanity Tales II: The
Sense of Fear,* © 2015 Books & Boos Press

Revisions edited by S& L Editing (slediting.com)

For Ms. Carol Lacoss, my sophomore high school English teacher. You managed to make Greek tragedy fun, and a visit to Dante's *Inferno* one hell of a ride.

CONTENTS

SECRET THINGS

I suppose all married couples have secrets.

My wife's secret is that she's smoking again. She has a cigarette in the morning on the way to the commuter lot before catching the bus to Hartford, to the lawyer's office where she works as a paralegal. After the long ride home, most of which is taken up with sitting in traffic on I-84, she stands in the parking lot and takes a moment to enjoy a second smoke break. She justifies it by telling herself *if I only have two, I'm not really smoking again*, but she feels the need to hide it just the same. She lights up quickly, secretively—looking around to see if anyone she recognizes might still be in the lot, waiting to report her filthy habit to her hapless husband. Once the nicotine has soothed her, she drives home to the drudgery of making me dinner, taking a shower, and preparing for work the next day. She spritzes herself with lavender Febreze and chews a couple of peppermint Mentos on the way home to cover up the smell, in the hopes that I won't notice.

Maybe, in other circumstances, this'd be enough to keep me in the dark.

This is not Gretchen's only secret. Sometimes, when we're making love, she pretends I'm someone else. It didn't happen right away—not for the first year of our marriage, at least. But sometime during that second year, after reading a news article about her ex-boyfriend from high school, the one that wound up purchasing a sports team, that's when she started. Once in a while, she'd imagine that it wasn't me, average Joe Simmons, on top of her, but Mark Jacques, new owner of the Cheshire Cougars. And if we happen to go out for date night and catch a Vin Diesel movie? Forget it. I might as well not even show up for sex later that night; she's having a party all on her own.

We live in a house we can barely afford in South Glastonbury, right down the road from the Audubon Society, a delightful destination. The exhibits and photos don't interest me much, but whenever Gretchen wants to spend an afternoon there, I usually agree to walk down with her. There's a real pretty cemetery behind the Audubon, and while she's admiring the bird pictures, I like to stroll out back and read the tombstones, imagining what sort of lives the deceased led before winding up six feet under behind a feathered preserve. Were they farmers? Grocers? How did they end up here, in an upper-scale New England town, buried in a quiet grove that passersby probably don't even know exists?

Is this where I'll be buried someday?

Gretchen is hiding a doozy of a secret, you see. For the past eight months, she's been having an affair with

Lance Hartley, one of the attorneys for whom she works. It started innocently enough, a flirtation that ended in a kiss at the holiday party, the one I couldn't go with her to last December because of a nasty stomach bug. Since then, they've been working late together, waiting until the floor clears out as their coworkers go home one by one, before meeting in his office. They've had sex on the black leather couch, on his polished mahogany desk with the etched glass inlay, even up against his tasteful slate-blue wallpaper. He buys her gifts, too. Tokens of his appreciation: a pair of diamond earrings here, a jade bracelet there. Gretchen keeps them tucked away in a white silk drawstring bag she keeps hidden in her nightstand drawer, underneath her vibrator. She thinks I'll never look there, and truth be told, I haven't.

Gretchen just found out she's pregnant. This is going to be particularly difficult for her to explain, as I had a vasectomy two years ago after we decided children were definitely not something we wanted to pursue. It seems my Gretchen has had a change of heart on the matter. Turns out she wants children after all . . . just not with me.

To her credit, she isn't going to try and pass this child off as the result of a faulty snip job. She just doesn't think I'll buy it, and she's not thrilled at the idea of lying to both the child and to me for the rest of our lives. But she needs to do something soon, because she's already three months along and she won't be able to hide her growing midsection much longer.

So she has decided to murder me.

Divorce is not an option in Gretchen's mind. I bought the house before I met her, around the same time that I set up my psychiatry practice in town. She has no assets to her name—even the car she drives is registered to me—and she's afraid she'll walk away with nothing. After all, she's the one who cheated, and the evidence of that will be quite visible as the months in divorce court drag on. But if I were to meet an untimely end, she'd get it all—the house, the cars, and a substantial life insurance policy we set up as newlyweds, me never thinking that this nest egg would provide just enough motivation to tip my wife's hand toward homicide.

Gretchen has purchased a jar of ground glass from an arts and crafts store and plans to mix it in the stroganoff sauce she's preparing for dinner tonight. She'll wait until I'm too far gone to save and then rush me to the hospital. I've suffered from bleeding ulcers the past few years, so she's gambling the doctors will attribute my internal woes to this. After I die, she'll tell everyone the memories of our time together in Glastonbury are too much to bear, and pack up immediately for a new town and a new life with Lance. She likes Simsbury; she thinks Cheshire might be a nice place to live, too. She'll worry about that later.

Why she thinks the texture of the glass-laden stroganoff will not set off alarm bells for even the most indiscriminating of palates is beyond me. I'm a little disappointed in her, really—I thought she was more creative than that. And she's forgetting one important part of her happily ever after, which is that Lance should be a willing participant, too. He doesn't even know she's pregnant yet, and I happen to know he has no intention of leaving his wife and the two daughters he already has for Gretchen. But Lance need not worry.

You see, I have a few secrets of my own.

My first secret is that I was not entirely truthful when Gretchen asked me how my first wife died. I told her that Lisa accidentally drowned in the tub after having too much to drink and passing out in the bath. That was not exactly the whole story. Maybe "drowned after I held her under the bathwater until she stopped breathing" would be a little more accurate. And I know Gretchen plans to take a hot bath tonight, just to soothe her nerves before whipping up her specially prepared stroganoff.

My other secret is that I can read minds.

GOOD NIGHT, FRANCINE

Francine Campbell shuffled down her paved driveway early Saturday morning to retrieve the newspaper, much as she had every morning of her adult life, which, at seventy-six years old, was a substantial number of mornings. She was still attractive for an old biddy, she thought with a smile, and pulled the flaps of her robe in a little closer to her petite frame as she made her way down the walk. The robe was a gift from her nephew, and the blue piping along the pristine white terrycloth matched the cornflower blue of her eyes. Francine's hair had come in a brilliant white as she'd aged, and she faithfully had it permed into a tight cap of curls every eight weeks. Just as women of a certain age *should*, she figured.

Francine retrieved the *Bulletin* from her mailbox and paused. Her neighbor Annabel was out raking in the yard across the street. Francine raised her hand in greeting, and Annabel smiled and waved in return. Francine nodded, satisfied that Annabel had no suspicion that the sweet little lady across the street was the source of her repeated visits from the state's child and family services agents.

Francine liked Annabel and her husband Brian well enough; it was their two little brats that drove her nuts. Francine toiled every spring to plant her vegetable garden, making sure the rows were even and the plants were spaced apart exactly as instructed on the package. Last summer, she'd spied Benny and Brenda in among her plants, picking worms off of her tomatoes and squealing in delight as they squished them. Her tomatoes had not ripened quite right that July, staying tinged with orange instead of ripening to a robust red, and Francine just *knew* the disruption of those unruly little monsters was to blame. She had taken to anonymously calling the state whenever she spotted them covered in dirt after a day's play or if she overheard a loud fight across the street. *Diligence*, she thought, turning back up the driveway, the word as comforting as a fresh-baked roll. If she was diligent with her phone calls, those imps would be out of the neighborhood before too long.

Francine made her way back to the house, an old colonial with stone walls that her great-grandfather had built for his small family. Except for the two years during which she'd lived in the dorms while attending the Hartford College for Women, Francine had spent her whole life in this house. She loved every granite rock forming its foundation, and she'd been pleased when the state had purchased the gravel pit abutting the property, preserving the land and freeing her from the worry of nosy next-door neighbors. Sometimes at night Francine heard the rumble of dirt bike motors from local teenagers off-roading in the old pits, and it irritated her to no end. Francine liked to walk the paths from time to time, dropping handfuls of nails along the trails in the hopes that a teenage hoodlum or two might be deterred from their hooting and hollering by a flat tire.

It wasn't just the teenagers that were the problem. Oh, no. Parents from all over the neighborhood allowed their spoiled terrors to run rampant in the gravel pits, unsupervised, causing a ruckus and scaring away the birds and squirrels. Francine clenched her jaw at the thought. This was the reason she left the abandoned refrigerator in her yard, back in the bushes near the property line of the state land. Her dad had dumped it out there when Francine was away at school, and although there was a law stating the door had to come off of the weathered green appliance, neither Francine nor her father had ever bothered to take it off its hinges. Francine left the door ajar, checking it every so often in the hopes that some snooping child playing hide-and-seek in the pits would find it and lock themselves in.

She'd yet to find any suffocated bodies in there, but she kept hoping.

Francine found it absurd that any decent parent would let their children play in the pits. As a child, her own mother and father had warned her and her brother John not to wander next door, for fear that a landslide of gravel would bury them alive. And despite John's warnings, his wife Betsy had picnicked in the pits at least twice a week in the summer when they were newly married and Francine's nephew Louie was just a baby. It was a tragedy waiting to happen, Francine knew. Betsy had gotten exactly what she deserved when the sand had started sliding down toward her little picnic, collapsing on top of her as she struggled to climb out of the pit. She'd cried out as the gravel filled her mouth, calling her husband's name before disappearing beneath the dirt. Francine's spirit warmed with smug satisfaction every time she recalled the woman's death cries. She'd hated Betsy from the first day they'd met, and when that little harlot had trapped her beloved brother into marrying her by seducing him and getting knocked up, well, Francine had bided her time. She knew how tenuous the gravel pit walls were, and it had only taken a little weight—oh so carefully nudged, so as not to get caught in the slide herself—to set the avalanche in motion.

Francine had hoped she and her brother would grow close again after she'd buried Betsy alive, but John had been devastated by the death of his young wife. He'd packed up his son, moving out of the family home and clear across town. He'd never remarried, and Louie himself was a grown man now, working landscaping jobs around town, occasionally stopping by to mow his spinster aunt's lawn and visit a spell.

It was Louie whom Francine was off to visit today. Her nephew had hinted several times that he would love to inherit the old stone house once Francine passed away, and she was going to meet Louie for lunch and give him a copy of her will. She'd left the old homestead to her nephew in her final testament, and she knew it would make his day. He'd probably be over every weekend now to help fix up the property and update the plumbing. Francine had signed the deed of her property over to the local Volunteers for Animals three years ago, with the

10

proviso that she be granted a lifelong lease to the home. Francine would be happy to leave her house to Louie— but of course, she couldn't give away what wasn't legally hers anymore. Her only regret was that she wouldn't be able to see his devastated expression when he found out his aunt had deceived him. Unless, of course, there really *was* an afterlife. The thought of coming back as a ghost to haunt Louie tickled Francine, and she giggled as she pulled a Pepto-Bismol-pink velour sweatshirt over her thin shoulders.

Louie had been an all-right-enough nephew for the most part, helping her with the lawn, and driving her to all of her appointments the time she broke her foot tripping on a rock whilst sprinkling nails on the gravel pit trails. But in all the years she'd bought him gifts for his birthday, holidays, even sending him a crisp five dollar bill from time to time when he was at college, Louie had never bothered to send her a thank-you note. Not one written word of thanks in fifty years, and Francine just couldn't abide such rudeness. There was no way that little ingrate was going to get her beloved family home!

Francine drove her Lexus into town, stopping by the Sup-R-Mart for her cholesterol medication and a bag of pork rinds. She so enjoyed pork rinds with a cup of lemon zinger tea as a late afternoon snack. When the rinds rang up on sale at the checkout counter, Francine smiled at the young man bagging her purchases before she could stop herself.

"Walk these out to your car, ma'am?" the boy asked, half grinning, encouraged by Francine's apparent good mood. The corners of Francine's mouth turned down so sourly the boy's pierced brow wrinkled in confusion.

"Absolutely *not*, you little thief. Trying to make a buck off helping a decrepit old lady, are you? I didn't fatten my mattress by handing out tips to rotten freeloaders like you, that's for sure!" The young man's mouth was agape, and she snatched her grocery bag from his hand. "I'm perfectly capable of carrying my own groceries, thank you. What a clever little shyster you are," she added, storming off to the exit. Francine hated to be taken advantage of, and she hadn't expected it from the bag boy. She was still a little shaken as she drove to the restaurant to meet Louie.

"You okay, Aunt Frannie?" Louie asked as he opened her car door for her. "You seem a little rattled."

"I'm fine," she snapped.

Louie had lost most of his hair, save for a sprinkle around the base of his skull that had more gray than blond these days. He had a paunchy stomach and wore a yellow polo shirt that pulled tight across his gut, straining to stay tucked into his tan Dickies. He offered his arm to his aunt, and strolled with her to the restaurant entrance, holding the door. Francine settled into the booth, forcing herself to breathe deeply and calm down. After all, she was here to brighten her nephew's day, and once he saw the copy of the will, she was sure he'd offer to pick up the tab for lunch. Maybe she'd order dessert, too. She would *not* let a thieving bagboy ruin her free meal.

"Did you go to that new dentist I told you about?" Louie asked over breadsticks. Their old family dentist, Dr. Greenleaf, had passed away unexpectedly, and she and Louie had been looking for a replacement ever since. "Isn't Dr. Chang nice?"

Dr. Chang was *not* nice, and had made a comment to Francine that she needed to take better care of her teeth now that she was reaching her twilight years, unless she wanted to check out the latest in denture apparel. Francine had not appreciated his comments on her dental hygiene, and had made it a point to return to Dr. Chang's waiting room on a busy Friday afternoon and make herself comfortable on his cushy ivory sofa in the lobby. Francine had then urinated on his couch, stood, and left. The receptionist had even smiled at the short, slightly stooped, grandmotherly old woman when she left. The idea that Francine might need to floss more was ridiculous. She'd find another dentist, one who appreciated her fine brushing skills.

"Aunt Frannie? You still with me?" Francine winced at the nickname, one her brother had teased her with growing up and Louie had picked up on as soon as he could talk. Frannie was a fat girl's name. *She* was Francine. She looked at her nephew watching her with a puzzled smile. Francine decided not to share her sofa story with Louie, and pulled her will out of her purse.

"I have a little surprise for you, dear," she said, beaming. "No point in giving you a gift if I can't see how much you'll enjoy it." She tried to suppress a chuckle; this was priceless.

As Louie read the will leaving Francine's home to her beloved nephew, tears formed in his eyes. "Thank you, Aunt Frannie—thank you so much!" *Sure,* now *he thanks me,* Francine thought with a frown. *Would it kill you to put it in writing? A note card, maybe, or even a postcard?* She hoped the Volunteers for Animals would make a nice kennel out of her living room.

"How's your father?" Francine asked, sipping her diet iced tea with lemon. Her beloved brother, two years her senior, had been suffering from Alzheimer's for almost a decade now. The nursing home he was in had slowly drained away all of John's and Louie's assets, and the hope was now that John would pass away sooner rather than later, before Louie was forced to sign over the three-room condominium in which he now lived.

"Dad has his good days and his bad. Mostly bad. Have you been by to see him lately?"

"Just last week," Francine lied. She hadn't been to visit her brother in years, but wasn't like John could tattle on her anymore. "He didn't recognize me at all."

"Yeah." Louie sighed, nodding. "He asked me yesterday if I was there to fix the television. He wanted it working before Andy Griffith came on." Louie stabbed a french fry with his fork and shook his head. "It really would be a blessing if he'd give up the ghost." A sad frown played across his lips. Francine wondered if her nephew would say that about *her* now as well, since he thought the house was as good as his. She clenched her teeth and tucked in to her lunch, a chicken Florentine dish that promised to put her cholesterol through the roof.

Louie held her elbow after lunch, escorting her to the door. He had indeed paid for the meal, insisting it was the least he could do after her incredibly generous gift. Francine patted Louie's arm.

"You go on ahead, dear. I left my car keys in the booth." Louie nodded and kissed her cheek, and Francine turned back to where they'd been sitting. She put her purse on the seat and slid the ten dollars Louie had left for the waitress into her pocketbook. Her tea had had entirely too much lemon in it, and she would be damned if that tired-looking waitress was going to be rewarded for her poor service.

***

That evening, Francine settled down to read a few chapters of the Agatha Christie novel she'd picked up last week at the library book sale. At 9:30 PM exactly—Francine was diligent about her bedtime—she clicked off the light on her nightstand and shut her eyes, satisfied with the day.

She dozed peacefully for a couple of hours, until the creaking of the floorboards in the kitchen startled her awake. She blinked a few times, then sat up, alarmed.

There was someone in the house. Francine was sure of it. She could smell stale cigarette smoke. She held her breath and stared into the darkness. She'd left her screen windows open due to the evening being so warm, and silently cursed herself as she listened.

There. Soft footsteps in the kitchen. Someone was definitely in her home.

Francine inhaled deeply, trying not to panic. She had moved her bed into one of the rooms on the main floor a couple of years ago, figuring the day might come when she wouldn't be able to navigate the stairs so easily. But she was still a spry old bird, she knew, and began to mentally assess the room. Hide in the closet? No, too obvious, and she'd be too easy to spot. She kept her closet neatly organized, all her clothes ironed and arranged by color. Her shoes hung in tidy pairs from a shoe rack over the closet door. There was nothing for her to hide behind, in, or under.

The window. She could stand on her mattress and climb out the window over the bed's backboard. She was wearing lavender silk pajamas—she'd put them on because they would keep her cool throughout the night's heat, but she realized now they were also pretty practical to wear when one had to scramble out the window. She stood on the bed and leaned to the screen, slowly pulling in the tabs that would allow the mesh frame to move. *Careful now, careful . . .*

Francine worked the frame up the runners bit by bit, not wanting to alert the intruder to the fact that she was awake. She heard him in the den now, slowly making his way around the room. She saw a beam of light out in the hallway, probably from a flashlight. The intruder seemed to be in no hurry to just grab her valuables and get out. This behavior terrified Francine. Why wasn't he just snatching her television and running?

At last Francine worked the screen up high enough to squeeze her body through. She leaned over further, lifting her left leg and swinging it out the window so she straddled the sill. She started ducking her head through the window, and looked back into a bright, blinding beam of light. The intruder had found her room, caught her mid-flight.

"Where do you think you're going, you miserable bat? Get back here!" Francine blinked, pushed herself out the window, and jumped.

She landed on the hard ground on her rump, and sat, stunned, for just a moment. Then Francine stood and ran.

She'd caught a glimpse of the intruder's head and hand as he poked out the window. He held a long knife, like she'd seen the fishermen use at the beach to fillet their catch. Francine knew she was running for her life.

Her knees were not what they used to be, throbbing as she sprinted across the lawn toward the gravel pits. If she could lead him in there, she might be able to double up back behind him, and trick him into one of the pits, maybe start a slide . . .

No, you can't, Francine, she thought with a shock. She heard her pursuer behind her, brushing off his pants after jumping out the window, and realized he wasn't hurrying. She couldn't run as fast as she used to, and was breathing so hard from her sprint toward the back she'd given herself a sharp pain in her side. He wouldn't have any trouble catching up with her.

She was fighting time, gravity, and age. She wasn't going to make it to the pits.

Francine slowed slightly, looking around for a place to hide. Her pajamas were light in color, and would be easy to spot in the brush. The old refrigerator, tucked in to the bushes behind the shed, caught her eye. Salvation! Francine loped over to the old hulking appliance and climbed in. She fit snugly, and pulled the door closed slowly, careful to hold it ajar by curling her bony fingertips between the door and the latch. She tried to calm her breathing, which was coming out in ragged jags. Francine tried to meditate—*breathe in four counts, breathe out for four,* she told herself, remembering an article on relaxation techniques she'd read in *Women's Day*. Francine focused on her inhalations, trying not to panic at the notion that someone had broken into her home with the intent to . . . well, to hurt her. She thought again of the knife. Really, to kill her.

Who would want to do this to her?

What had she ever done to anyone?

For a moment she thought of the bag boy at the Sup-R-Mart, the one she had called a shyster. Hadn't she as much as told him she kept her money in her mattress? *Stupid, stupid mistake, Francine*, she berated. It could be him; he'd looked a little malicious, for a teenage bag boy. *Or Louie*, she thought with a fright. Maybe he'd gone to the town assessor's office to appraise his future property and found out it wasn't his aunt's to give away.

Francine heard a low chuckle right outside the refrigerator door. She pulled her fists to her mouth, pressing hard to keep herself from screaming.

When she did, the last sound Francine Campbell heard in all her seventy-six years was the soft click of the refrigerator door as it latched shut.

TIME TO LET GO

It's early, and still dark, but Ben has his room memorized. He sits up in the gloom, rubbing his cheeks to wake up. He pulls on a neatly pressed shirt and dress pants, slaps on a little cologne—*Joop!*, something one of his past girlfriends bought him, which he still wears and now considers his signature scent. He doesn't bother with a light, just pulls on his sneakers and makes his way outside, to see what the world has to offer today.

Ben doesn't work—doesn't need to. His family provides everything he requires, so he usually spends his days roaming the wooded area behind his home. He likes to think of himself as a sort of nature survivalist. *Into the Wild* by Jon Krakauer was one of his favorite books when he was younger, and he can empathize with the main character, the guy who died trying to make it on his own in the wilderness. Ben would do that too, except that he really likes the creature comforts of things like his own plush pillow. He doesn't mind spending the day among the pine trees and squirrels, but he always finds himself heading home again to the familiar coziness of his four walls when dusk falls.

The ladies like Ben—always have. His scruffy blond hair and hoarfrost eyes have made many a teenage girl swoon, and he had his fair share of romances in college. He isn't seeing anyone special now; hasn't for a long time, not since he walked in on his girl, Janna, on her knees in front of his now former best friend Jimmy. It's taking him some time to get over Janna—he really thought she was the one he was going to marry. It's why he spends so much time walking in the woods, meditating on his life. He *knows* he needs to get over her and move on, but he can't help replaying every detail of their relationship, wondering what he could have done differently. Bought her flowers more often, maybe. Let her pick the movie once in a while.

Ben hikes into the woods, huffing a little as he climbs a hill near a pebbly slope. The rocks are next to a small clearing of tall grass that turns yellow and brittle in late summer. He likes to sit on the stones and study the woods, waiting for the deer to step into the clearing and graze. There's a fat woodchuck that burrows under the stones at night; during the day, Ben watches him waddle out into the field, digging for edible roots. Ben has mastered the art of sitting without making the faintest sound, which is what he decides to do now, squatting his lanky frame down on a cold gray boulder, folding his legs Indian-style.

Ben is watching the woods with increasingly heavy lids when a woman in a filmy ivory dress steps out from the tree line. She slowly makes her way to the rocks on light feet, seeming to glide over the grass. A half-smile—*an inner smile*, Ben thinks—rests on her face. She places a perfectly manicured pink hand on the rocks and starts to climb. She's almost on top of him when Ben clears his throat.

"Oh!" she yelps, sitting down hard. All illusion of grace is extinguished when she thumps her tailbone. Tears form in her eyes as she looks up at him from where she has plopped down. Her eyes go wide. "Ben? Is that you?"

Ben studies the woman's face. She has curly red hair and a small scar above her left eyebrow. It's his friend Holly, from college. Janna's roommate. He can't remember the last time he's seen her. She looks like she may have put on a few pounds.

"Holly. Fancy meeting you here." His smile becomes a laugh. Really, this is ridiculous. They're in a field in the woods in a town at least a hundred miles from the state university they both attended. It's been two years since graduation. Ben remembers that he always felt uncomfortable around Holly. If she got a few drinks in her—and she *liked* to drink, a little too much and too often—she would drape her arm over him, lean in until he could feel her hot breath on his cheek, and ask him in a whisper why he was with someone like Janna when he could do better. She knew a *few* people who were better girlfriend material than Janna. Herself included. Ben shakes off the memory, but not before wondering for a moment if she is stalking him.

"My God. Ben." Holly's voice trembles. Her lip quivers, as if she's about to burst into a full-blown crying jag.

"What're you doing here? And why are you wearing a dress in the woods?" he asks, hoping to distract her from the impending tears. She blinks at him. Looks down at the delicate ivory sheath in which she has just traipsed through the forest. Meets his gaze again and laughs, a short bark, as if her own wardrobe stumps her.

"I was just at the church." She gestures in a half-hearted wave toward where she'd emerged at the south end of the clearing. She looks around at the rocks where they're sitting, lets her eyes drift to the field for a moment before letting them return to his face. Ben can feel her staring at his hair, his lips. He clears his throat before her gaze can devour him.

"Faith Congregational?" he asks, the name coming to him out of smoke. He knows the church, but can't quite remember why.

"Yes, that's right," she says, a little dreamily. "I'm getting married."

"Married! Who's the lucky guy? Anyone I know?"

"Nick Bates," Holly says, voice cracking. "He's a nice guy; really; he is. I met him the month before graduation. At the library, studying for finals. His family is from here, so I moved with him after. Nick's a nice guy," Holly repeats, sighing. "But I don't think I can go through with it." She squints, leaning toward Ben. "Truth be told, when I was getting ready this morning, I found myself thinking about you."

"Me?" Ben feels the goose bumps rise on the back of his neck, then realizes she is probably teasing him. "Not funny, Holly."

"No, Ben, *not* funny. None of this is funny. I just left a man who's crazy about me at the altar, because the memory of my long-gone roommate's long-gone boyfriend made me realize that I'm not ready to get married to anyone. Not until I deal with my feelings for you. I sure did miss you, Ben." She smiles. "It really is great to see you. Ironic, but great."

Ben doesn't know how to respond. If she's been carrying a torch for him all this time, well, she might be crazy. She might hurt herself, he realizes, his stomach clenching.

Or him.

He studies her face. She doesn't *look* homicidal. Her skin is smooth, almost ethereal. He wonders how she got that thin white line snaking off her eyebrow, and then remembers: a fall in the bathtub. She was five. He must have asked her before.

"Holly," he starts, then pauses. "How did you find me out here, anyway?"

"It's not like I was *looking* for you—that's just insane! I bolted from the church," she explains. "As soon as I got outside, I caught the faintest whiff of *Joop!* in the breeze. Of course it reminded me of you, although I knew in the back of my mind that it couldn't possibly be. You. But look. Here you are." She leans in, pats his hand. Slowly strokes it for a moment. It feels good, and Ben doesn't pull away. Why is it that he and Holly never got together? That's right. He frowns. Because he was utterly, thoroughly, blindly in love with Janna. Janna, who loved his best friend. Many, many times, behind his back.

"I guess I should've listened to you about Janna," he offers as an apology. Holly nods slowly.

"I just hated seeing you with her. She was terrible to you, you know." And Ben does know. He knows Jimmy was not the first. He remembers walking into Janna and

Holly's apartment one morning, the air in the living room heavy with cigarette smoke, to find Janna and Holly talking to Eric, a communications major in Janna's film class. Eric was wearing underwear and a tee shirt and Ben had been alarmed that he could see Eric's junk through the flap of his boxers. Janna had whispered to Ben that Holly had hooked up with Eric the night before; the girls were just making him a little breakfast before sending him on his way. But it was *Janna* Eric was sitting close to on the couch. Ben had sensed it then, that Janna was lying, but he didn't want to believe it. Couldn't.

"I don't want to talk about her," Ben says, shaking his head. He leans in toward Holly, who is smoothing the gossamer fabric of her gown. "She was . . . what about you? What are you up to these days?"

Holly shrugs. "I'm working at an insurance company, investigating claims. Making a life with Nick. Thinking about you every once in a while. I was nuts about you, you know," she admits, and takes his hand again.

"You didn't really hide it, Holly." He grins, then allows his face to settle into what he hopes is a serious frown. "But listen. You can't go through life pining after me. You and I, well, we weren't ever going to be together. You're a lot of fun, Holly, but I never really felt that way about you. You were just Janna's friend, that's all. And it might not be fair, but all of those murky, angry thoughts about Janna that I still have, well, they kind of carry over to you. I'm sorry," he adds, because her eyes have filled and he can see that he has hurt her feelings. "It's just the way it is."

Holly abruptly stands, turning her face away from him. Her shoulders shudder. Ben hears her breathe heavily, shakily; then she turns back to him:

"I guess that's fair." Her voice jitters. "I can't ask you to say you were secretly in love with me or anything. You're allowed to feel the way you feel." She draws in another deep breath. "I probably needed to hear that anyway. Maybe that's why I'm here. Like you said, I can't carry a torch for you forever."

Ben stands with her, brushing off his pants. He holds his arms out, and she walks in to them. They hug, solidly, for a minute.

"I don't know that we'll see each other again," he muses. "Probably not. I *do* wish you well, though. I want you to be happy."

She pulls back, looks into his eyes with a watery smile. "Thanks. You too," she whispers.

Holly makes her way off the rocks, slowly winding her way through the field. She turns to look back at him, raises her hand in a half wave, and disappears through the trees once again.

***

Ben decides to follow her from a safe distance. There's a slim chance Janna could be at the wedding, though he suspects this is doubtful. He has a sense that their friendship ended—possibly because of him. Still, his curiosity is overwhelming. He *has* to look. Holly is hurriedly making her way back to the church. Good. Looks like she's going through with it after all.

"Where did you go?" her groom asks from the doorway. He wears a mask of worry, and there's a tremble to the hand that nervously stubs out a cigarette at Holly's approach. Holly shakes her head.

"I took a walk in the woods. I needed to clear my head. I panicked. I'm sorry," she says, and the tears fall.

"Are you okay now?" Nick asks, rubbing her back.

"I think so. I ran into someone in the woods. My friend Ben." Nick wrinkles his forehead. From his spot in the shadows of the tree line, Ben sees concern in Nick's eyes.

"Ben? The same Ben who shot and killed your roommate and then himself two years ago?"

"That's the one." Holly sighs. "I *know* you think I'm crazy, but it was him. I touched him, and he was really there. He told me to move on with my life. And he's right. I do need to move on. With you." She snakes her hand through the crook of Nick's arm, and lets him escort her into the church.

***

Back on the rocks, Ben watches the sun dip to the horizon. Janna was nowhere to be found among the ghosts at the wedding. She's probably lost to him forever now, but still, he searches. He strolls through the field, careful not to disturb the woodchuck sitting on its haunches. Ben makes his way back home and climbs into his casket, settling into his grave for the evening.

CLIFFHANGER

For their fifth wedding anniversary, Victor and Holly Shaw decided to celebrate at the Grand Canyon. Over the past five years, they'd bought a new home, sold it at a loss after Victor was laid off, and bought a smaller home with Victor's signing bonus from his new firm. They'd buried his mother and put her father in a nursing home once the Alzheimer's had become too much to handle. They'd fought over finances and reconciled over their shared dream to ride cross-country on a pair of Harleys someday. Overall, Holly Shaw was feeling blessed and very much in love with her husband this June morning, taking in the sienna view of the canyon at Mather Point.

"Unbelievable," Holly breathed, trying to wrap her mind around the colors and layers she was seeing. "It's like a whole cross-section of Mother Earth, laid bare and vulnerable for us to worship."

"Can't you just say it's amazing and leave it at that?"

27

Victor grumbled. "Honestly, Holly. Now I've got an image of someone's mom being hacked to death. Gross." He made a face and peered over the security fence, down at the jagged gorge. Victor looked sideways at her and winked. He brought his leg over the low fence and was suddenly standing on the other side, with nothing between him and the canyon to stop him from plummeting over. "Come on, Holly Hobby. Let's take a closer look."

"Victor! Cut it out!" Holly squealed, but she was already following him. He was only carrying out what she'd wanted to do anyway. It was one of the things she loved about him—he was a rule-breaker.

She came up alongside of him and looked down. The height of their perch as she gazed into the magnificent crevice that lay gaping before her made her head dizzy. With a shaky, smile, Holly glanced up to look at Victor—and suddenly lost her footing. She screamed, sliding down the sheer cliff beneath her, her hands scrambling at the air, finding no purchase. Holly twisted her body toward the earth, desperate to hold on. She cried out and her mouth filled with dirt and pebbles. The skin on her face shredded as she tried desperately to cling to the side of the rock wall.

Certain she was about to die, it took Holly a moment to realize she'd stopped moving. Her toes had a shaky grasp on a thin shelf, about five inches wide. She reached up with her left hand and grabbed a scrubby branch snaking out the side of the cliff. Now that she was more firmly secured, Holly immediately wet her pants, then started to cry.

"Holly? Oh my God, Holly!"

Holly's cheek was pressed to the side of the rock wall,

and as she tried to push herself flat against it, she slowly angled her face upward toward the sound of her husband's voice. Victor paced at the top of the ravine, trying to peek over the side to see her without losing his footing.

"Victor? Victor, I'm okay. Go get help! Help me!" She could barely see him, and guessed she'd fallen about 300 feet. Her face was on fire, and she figured she had some serious road rash from sliding down the side of a rock cliff. Nothing felt broken, and she was able to stand upright, though the tiny shelf was already making her feet cramp.

"I'm going back to the visitor's center," Victor shouted. "I'll get the park rangers. Hang tight, honey. Everything will be fine. Oh, God, Holly." Victor's face disappeared, and Holly sighed. As far as anniversary trips went, this one was turning out to be pretty sucky.

Holly and Victor had met at a biking fundraiser six years ago. She'd been fresh from her divorce from her first husband, a worthless excuse of a man who'd quit his job the day after they'd gotten married and refused to get out of the La-Z-Boy after that. She'd stuck it out with him for three years before finally having enough, and once her divorce was final, she swore she'd never get married again. But then she'd caught sight of Victor, with his shaved head and auburn goatee, gently wiping the fingerprints off of his Harley at the Ride to Cure Multiple Sclerosis. Her stomach had squeezed in a flip-floppy dance the moment she'd laid eyes on him, and when he caught her staring, he'd broken out in a dimpled smile and strolled over to greet her.

Holly was a strikingly attractive woman. She had honey blonde hair and wide green eyes, and a metabolism most would kill for. She wore very little makeup and was often unaware of the effect she had on men. She'd gone to the MS Ride with her neighbor Brenda, who had talked Holly into coming with her in an effort to 'spice up' their social lives. Brenda had elbowed Holly as Victor approached, and both women giggled more like schoolgirls than the thirtysomethings they actually were.

"What's a nice gal like you doing in a place like this?" Victor had drawled, and Holly'd rolled her eyes. He'd been wearing a leather vest and jeans that hugged him in all the right places, and for a moment she'd wondered if he was gay, until she realized how intently he was admiring her breasts. He'd introduced himself and offered her a ride on his bike, and over coffee later, when she'd found out he was an accountant and lived with his ailing mother, she was already good and hooked. She was completely in love with Victor, and even now, after five years of marriage, he still made her blush with anticipation when he flashed his dimples in her direction.

Where *was* Victor? It seemed like he was taking forever to get help. Holly's toes were completely numb now, which worried her. She could easily lose her tenuous foothold on the little ridge. She carefully lifted her left foot, wiggled it around some to get the blood flowing, and set it back down sideways on the shelf. Now more of her foot was touching the ledge. She felt the prickliness in her feet and hoped that meant the feeling was returning. But wait—that wasn't just tingling. There was something else.

Holly slowly slid her head down to try and catch a glimpse of her left foot. A small, translucent scorpion was making its way up her shoe, tickling her ankle. She yelped and kicked, and the scorpion went sailing into the canyon.

The jerking motion caused her to wobble for a moment, and she pressed against the wall again, panting. Were there other arachnids around? Didn't they lay eggs in batches? Did that little guy have a bunch of scorpion brothers and sisters? She struggled to calm down, trying to remember her yoga breathing. The straggly branch she clung to with an iron grip shook uncontrollably. *Breathe in. Breathe out. Think of something calming, like ice cream cones at the beach.* Why hadn't they gone to the beach? Goddamn Victor and his stupid Grand Canyon idea. Holly shivered as she worked to become still again. She thought she felt all sorts of bugs crawling on her, and tried to think rationally. Sure, a whole herd of ticks, spiders, and scorpions could be creeping up her legs right now. As long as she didn't agitate them by moving, they wouldn't sink their poisonous little fangs in. Holly suddenly remembered reading somewhere that there was a type of fly that laid eggs under the human skin, the host completely unaware of the larvae growing and feeding on their flesh until an adult fly poked its antennae out. Where did those things live? Was it Africa? Or Arizona?

She was not doing a good job of calming herself down.

Where the hell was Victor? Jesus, that man was slow as a slug at times, but she'd thought perhaps *this* time, in *this* situation, he might actually break into a trot or something. His lackadaisical nature could be infuriating. There were times when drama and panicking were absolutely called for. Like right now. The fact that the situation called for a rescue squad, or a helicopter, or maybe even a SWAT team, should've made Victor a little more responsive. Honestly, that man!

He's a good guy, she thought, chastising herself. He

always came home with flowers on special anniversaries, like the day they'd moved in together, or the time he'd proposed. After all, this trip had been his idea, to celebrate their time together. Her only idea for celebrating their fifth had been dinner at Applebee's.

Victor worked long hours at the accounting firm and often had to go in on the weekends. Really, if she could change one thing about their marriage, it would be that. Holly worked as a paralegal for a lawyer's office, but she was very clear about separating her job from her home life. Victor didn't share that same dedication to a work/life balance. More than one family picnic or romantic outing had been cut short by Victor's pager, calling him back into the office.

And, Holly had to admit, since she was stuck on the side of a sheer cliff and possibly facing her own clumsy death, she wasn't crazy about Victor's boss. Andrea Bellows was a tall woman with angles like a cat, silky black hair and brilliant white teeth. Sweet as could be. Always asking Holly about her job and her father. Holly hated her guts for being so nice. And beautiful. *Let's face the truth, Holly Hobby. If she were your boss* you'd *even consider sleeping with her.* Victor and Andrea put in a lot of time together. *Really,* she realized with a frown, *Victor spends more time with her than he does with me.*

The revelation clamped an icy claw around her heart. Was her husband having an affair? Did it take a tiny ledge with cramped toes and a certainty that things were not going to end well today to see what was clearly right in front of her? When he wasn't at the office with Andrea, heads practically touching as they reviewed ledger sheets,

Victor was often on the phone with her, discussing a particularly bothersome account or tax return. Holly was amazed he'd been able to tear himself away from Andrea long enough to spend a week with his wife on vacation. Not that Andrea hadn't called the hotel twice already for his feedback on a big client being audited by the IRS.

Holly leaned into the cliff and started to cry. Her husband was cheating on her, she was sure of it now. He was gorgeous. Women hit on him all the time. Andrea was beautiful. They made a stunning couple—Holly closed her eyes and pictured them together, so handsome and well matched. Were his coworkers whispering about the affair? Did they feel bad for Holly, left hung out to dry on a ledge while Victor and Andrea laughed behind her back?

And now that she thought about it, hadn't she felt *something*—a tiny pulse of pressure, right on the small of her back—just before she fell?

Had Victor *pushed* her?

Her heart began to race as she replayed the morning's events in her head. She'd been bitching about the coffee in the hotel room, which tasted like boiled socks and halitosis. Victor used up all of the hot water in the shower, and she'd been particularly venomous about that. They'd gotten lost on the way to the Grand Canyon, which she may have implied only a lobotomized chimpanzee could do. The lecture in the visitor's center had been boring. She'd had a rock in her sneaker. Victor took a long time to pee in the bathroom before they'd set out into the park.

Oh, dear God. She was a shrew.

Wait a minute, she told herself, absentmindedly rolling her right ankle as she thought. *Sure, you've been a little cranky on this trip.* But honestly, there were a million signs pointing the way to the South Rim. It was almost like Victor had purposely tried to get them lost on the way to one of nature's most impressive achievements.

Maybe he was having second thoughts about murdering his wife.

Holly couldn't help it. She started to bawl. The more she thought about it, the more she was sure she'd felt a push on the base of her spine right before she fell. Now she was stuck on a tiny ridge overlooking a gigantic gaping hole in the earth's crust, and her husband had put her there. He clearly wanted her dead so he could be with Andrea. There were no park rangers coming, no rescue squad. No SWAT team. Eventually she would lose consciousness, be it from dehydration or scorpion sting. Victor was going to let her die.

Her shoulders shook as she sobbed, and the tiny branch she clung to pulled free. Holly trembled, dropping the useless branch and pressing her palms flat against the side of the canyon to steady herself. She was going to die; of that, she was sure. She wondered how long Victor would wait after her funeral before announcing his engagement to Andrea.

She idly deliberated how much Andrea made a year; if Victor would sell their little cape and buy a fancy home with his mistress. Oh, God—what would happen to Gilligan, their cat? What if Andrea was allergic? Tears seeped down her cheeks as she thought of her orange tabby in an animal shelter. She barely even heard the ranger shouting down to her, asking if she was all right.

"Hello?" she called out, then, as an afterthought, "Is somebody there?"

"Missus Shaw? I'm Dennis Cole. I'm a park ranger, here to help, ma'am. The rescue team is going to lower me down to you, and I'll get you safely back up. Think you can hold on a few more minutes?"

"Yes! Oh, God, thank you so much. Thank you. How did you find me?"

Holly was startled to see Victor's head poke over the side of the rim. "I'm right here, honey. Everything's going to be okay. You just hang on tight, hon. I love you!"

Holly gasped. She'd been sure she'd figured out his whole plan. The grieving widower, the supportive boss, a new life without her . . . Holly gulped. She'd never been more ashamed in her life. How could she possibly have thought such awful, terrible things about the man she loved? She was the worst, most horrible wife in the history of spouses.

The ranger scaled down the side of the cliff until he was next to Holly on her little ridge. He hooked a rope and harness around her, and the two of them were pulled up, inches at a time, back to safety. Holly sat, shamefaced, as the paramedics treated the scrapes on her cheek and fingers. She just wanted to get back to the hotel room, change her shorts, and love her wonderful husband.

"How long was I down there?" Holly asked, massaging her cramped feet and toes.

Ranger Cole looked at his watch. "About twenty minutes, ma'am, near as I can figure."

Holly blinked and looked at Victor, holding her hand. He'd been reluctant to let go of her since she'd made it back topside.

"Imagine it wasn't much fun for you, ma'am. Lots of

thoughts can go through a person's mind, 'specially if they think they're about to die. Let this be a lesson to you—those security fences are there for a reason," he scolded, wagging his finger at Holly and Victor.

Twenty minutes? Holly was shocked. Could it be? In twenty minutes, she'd condemned her husband as an adulterer and a murderer. She'd thought the most awful things about him, and here he was, trying to comfort her. He alternated between hugging her and rubbing a small circle in her skin.

Right in the small of her back.

JOSEPHINE

Josephine Castellano Cato stood tall, with her shoulders back, her spine straight. She wore her silver hair swept up in a perfectly sprayed beehive, the black strands that still remained at her temples accenting the upward severity of her hairdo. She did not walk so much as direct herself into a room, demanding that all eyes follow her. Yes, Josephine Castellano Cato was a magnificent-looking woman. Everyone at the Shady Brook Retirement Home said so.

Josephine had been born right after the stock market crash in 1929. Despite the added financial pressure that a new baby could bring, her parents had fared well, thanks to Daddy's bootlegging business. They had raised her in a brick and slate Georgian colonial west of Hartford, with an emerald lawn that Daddy paid an Irishman named Benny O'Connor to maintain. When Josephine was too young to know any better, she would follow Benny with his well-oiled push mower, pulling out fists full of freshly chopped grass from the piles Benny carefully raked together, breathing deep the prickly scent before tossing the clippings in the air, letting them fall in her silky black hair and cling to her dress. Mother had put a stop to such unladylike activities after the first clump of lawn fell out from the hem of Josephine's jumper, but Josephine still thought of Benny O'Connor every sunny Saturday when Shady Brook's lawn was freshly mown.

Mother and Daddy had worked hard to be accepted in their West Hartford community. They had the money to buy their way into the best country clubs, but their Italian heritage made them *persona non grata* in some circles. Mother and Daddy tried their best to raise their little girl in the same waspish manner as they saw their neighbors do, but even with her bright red tricycle and patent leather shoes, Josephine never quite seemed to fit in with the local kids. After her mother smacked her bottom one day for studying anthills in the driveway instead of playing tag with the neighborhood Presbyterians, Josephine made more of an effort to hide her outsider status from her family.

Her parents put her in Junior School, a fancy new private academy consisting of six rooms draped in horrid turquoise. Josephine was taller than her schoolmates, and a little shy; she often stayed inside during play time, burying herself in a book while her classmates went out to kick the can. It was only herself and serene Mrs. Greene in the aqua rooms during those times, until the day James Hughes came to Junior.

James was taller than Josephine, with eyes like a rainy sky and a shock of white-blond hair. When he smiled, Josephine could see he was missing a tooth, the third one back. And at playtime, as the other kids were squealing outside over newly discovered frogs and rocks, James stayed behind and slid into the seat next to her, leaning in.

"Whatcha reading?" he asked.

Josephine, too startled to talk, showed him the front cover of her book, a worn copy of *Alice's Adventures in Wonderland.* James grinned, and held up the book he'd had tucked under his arm. It was the same novel. "How far along are you?"

Josephine showed him, and the two of them talked about white rabbits and red queens for the rest of recess. By the end of the school day, Josephine was in love.

Josephine and James were best friends through middle school, swapping books, catching pollywogs in the pond behind the library, and whispering secrets about teachers and classmates in each other's ears. James was the last thing on Josephine's mind at night and the first thing she thought of when she opened her eyes. She was embarrassed that James might find out how head-over-heels she was about him, but he never seemed to mind spending time with her.

He also never tried to hold her hand or get fresh with her, either.

Once they moved up to high school, things changed. Josephine's parents insisted on sending her to an exclusive private high school. James went to public school, which caused Mother and Daddy to start murmuring about Josephine's friendship with the boy. After all, they expected their daughter to marry well, and it would only hurt her chances if she were slumming it with a boy whose family could not afford proper schooling.

Josephine and James took to writing secret letters. Josephine would check the mailbox as soon as she got home from school, hoping to see a square of the yellow lined paper he scrawled on. She'd send him notes full of awkward poems and promises to meet again after graduation. James' letters were always lighthearted and full of stories about the football team or his difficult geometry class. Not once did he pledge his undying love, and as the years dragged on, his letters were less and less frequent, until they dried up altogether, leaving Josephine heartbroken.

Josephine dated very little through high school. None of the boys who dared to ask out the statuesque beauty seemed to measure up, in her mind, to her beloved James. On the rare occasion when she went for ice cream with Nick Grattani from the Young Italian Americans Club, she would sit across from him in the booth, thinking how his twitchy eyes were not as kind as James's, or how his pale, hairy knuckles were not as soft. Nick Grattani, frustrated with Josephine's cold, distracted conversation, eventually stopped asking.

Josephine was at the town Apple Festival the fall after graduation with her schoolmate Annabel when she turned away from the cotton candy booth and found herself face to face with James. He was tanned and laughing, and her heart skipped a beat. He ran a quick hand over his cropped hair, and his broad white grin made impossible not to flash him a smile in return.

"Josephine!" he beamed, and she found herself tongue-tied. "You look beautiful!"

She patted her hair nervously, which was teased up into

a beehive. She vowed on the spot to wear her hair this way forever. She silently cursed herself for wearing her old brown sweater, and not the green one with sapphire buttons that Daddy had given her last Christmas. For a moment, thinking about how his letters had dropped off, she wanted to slap James, to sting him as much as he'd stung her by forgetting about her. But one look into his cobalt eyes melted her anger.

"James," she finally managed to breathe.

He held her by the elbow and escorted her away from the Apple Festival and Annabel before any of her parents' friends could see them and cluck their tongues. They strolled down a path to Wolcott Park, while James babbled on about his summer in Rhode Island, working as a lifeguard for a private country club. It was as if they'd never stopped talking, never grown apart. Josephine couldn't speak—she was afraid she would start crying for happiness. He was just as handsome and soft-spoken as she'd remembered.

He guided her to a covered bridge, and they peeked over the side, pointing out silvery flashes whenever a fish neared the surface. James leaned in close, put his arm around her waist like it was something they did every day, and tilted her chin up.

"Josephine," he murmured. "I'd forgotten how truly beautiful you are. Now that I've seen you again, I can't believe I ever let us fall away." He leaned in and kissed her, tentatively at first, then forcefully, and she responded, wanting to breathe him in, taste all of him.

He pulled away at last, shaking his head. "I shouldn't have done that," he said, and dropped his arms.

"No, no, you should have," Josephine laughed, all of her schooling on behaving like a proper young lady going over the bridge with the fish. "Let's do it again."

"You don't understand. I've enlisted. Boot camp is over, and I'm leaving for Korea on Monday."

Josephine's heart turned to granite and fell to her feet. James—*her* James! Here they were, reunited at last, and he was leaving! Her eyes filled with hot tears.

"You can't! I refuse to—you can't leave me. That's not fair!" She stomped her foot, feeling like a foolish child, and James shrugged.

"I'm sorry," he said, palms up, almost pleading, and Josephine spun on her heel and ran.

Josephine stayed in her room all that weekend, alternating between hating James for toying with her and weeping at the thought of him going off to war. Late Monday afternoon, she finally came out of her room, washed her face, and sat down to dinner with her parents. When Mother asked what on earth had gotten into her the past few days, Josephine icily cut her off, telling her it was not up for discussion. Dinner—rosemary pork chops with roasted potatoes and green beans—was eaten in silence.

Josephine wrote to James twice a week, filling her letters with tales of the new cinnamon bread being sold at the bakery in town, the new highway going in between West Hartford and New Haven. She speculated on all of the things they would do together when he came home, Marlon Brando movies and moonlight drives overflowing onto the page. But James wrote precious few letters from Korea, and what he sent was bleak. The days were hot and the nights cold. The mountains he climbed took his breath away, but their beauty was marred by the death surrounding him. His friends were dying. His soul was dying a little bit, too. *It's no* Alice in Wonderland, *Josephine*, he wrote. *I fear that this war is changing me, and I'll never be able to relate to those I left behind again.*

Except for you, Josephine hoped he would write, but he never did. Then, just as he had during their high school years, he stopped writing altogether.

Josephine was heartsick, and angry that she'd let James do this to her a second time. Didn't he know she lived for his letters? A word from him could carry her through weeks of loneliness. How could he let her down *again*?

It took almost two years of checking an empty mailbox and crying herself to sleep at night for Josephine to realize she could not wait around for James. It hit her with calm certainty, reading about prisoners of war in the paper one morning over a hot cinnamon bun, that he was not coming back to her any time soon. She clipped out the article and tucked it away, along with her hopes, into her keepsake box. Sal Cato at the public accounting firm where she worked as a secretary had been hinting around for months that he would like to buy her dinner sometime. Clearly, James didn't care if Sal bought her dinner or not. She decided to let him.

Sal's kisses didn't make her toes curl like the stolen kiss at the bridge had, but he had a good heart, and her parents firmly approved of his honest work and fine family upbringing. Sal's father was from the old country, and had settled in Farmington when Sal was just a baby, working as a private accountant for some businessmen in New York. The Catos, much like the Castellanos, had worked hard to buy their family's status, and Josephine's father had a Cheshire cat grin when he gave his daughter away to Sal at their gauzy church wedding. Josephine knew she'd made a fine match. But when Josephine and Sal went to bed that night, Josephine closed her eyes and pretended it was her beloved James on top of her.

They settled in Farmington and over time, four sons came along. Sal put his foot down when Josephine wanted to name their youngest after James. They argued long into the night, Josephine vowing to leave Sal as soon as James came back for her, voice dripping with venom, but Sal stood firm. Their fourth child was named Antonio.

Josephine was active in the PTA and the women's auxiliary. Over the years, she imagined what James might look like at 30, at 40 . . . at 50. When Sal died of a heart attack at 55, she went through the motions of mourning appropriately, sending out thank-you cards for casseroles and spending time with each of the children to help ease the raw pain of losing their father. Sal had never really had her heart, and she felt bad about that, but she did think they'd had a nice life together, despite the shadow of James. She was even a little bit grateful that James hadn't come back to her at a time when she would have had to break Sal's heart by leaving him.

With Sal gone, Josephine threw herself into volunteer work, sitting on the local library board, organizing community blood drives, and cofounding the League of Italian American Women Bowlers. As her hair became peppered with more silver than black, time took its toll, and after she lost her license and had trouble remembering where she lived, her sons and daughters-in-law finally made the decision to move her into Shady Brook. They brought her brochures and pictures, and took her over one Saturday for a tour, telling her how happy she'd be there. Josephine studied the faces of the other residents there as they walked through, always searching for her James.

**

Josephine was sitting in bed, smoothing the curled edges of an old newspaper clipping, when the nurse came in.

"It's lunchtime, Josephine." The nurse smiled. "Time to head to the cafeteria. Aren't you hungry?" She moved to fluff the pillows behind the beautiful older woman, hoping to get her moving.

Josephine let her eyes lift from the article she'd been poring over, as if she were looking for new information in the faded newsprint. She shook her head slightly. "I'd like to stay here today." She sighed. "I'm waiting for a friend, and I just know in my heart that today's the day he's going to come back to me."

The nurse shrugged. "What do you have there?" she asked, leaning over to see what Josephine was reading. "An article about Little Sal? Did he make the paper again?"

Josephine pulled the clipping in closer to her heart for a moment, then slowly held it out in her palm just enough for the curious RN to see. "Why, Josephine Castellano Cato. That's an old obituary. What are you doing, sulking over things you can't change? You know you can't dwell on the past. It's the here and now you have to live in. Go on now, let's get out of bed and get you in the lunch room among the living." The nurse pulled down the corner of Josephine's blanket, and was met with an iron grasp that she hadn't thought the woman possessed.

"No! You don't understand. There're reports on the news every day about prisoners of war and misidentified bodies. I just know this obituary isn't true. You wait and see. My James is coming back to me."

The nurse stared at Josephine, open-mouthed. The obituary was from 1952. Surely this woman hadn't been waiting . . . all this time?

Josephine noticed nothing. She tucked the clipping into her worn copy of *Alice's Adventures in Wonderland*, content to wait for that boy with eyes the color of a rainy sky, who would surely come back for her.

Some day.

LOVE STINKS

Peter had been one of the shambling undead for a little over a month now, and Annie was running out of cows. Her father had originally estimated their herd at sixty head, but she'd quickly realized the first time she had to milk the cows by herself that Dad had overinflated that number. She had started out milking about forty-eight head, and with Peter eating a cow brain a day, she was down to just fourteen Holsteins.

Annie knew it wasn't an emergency yet—she still had the pigs, after all, and an assortment of barn cats—but she didn't know what she was going to do come fall. She shook her head in frustration as she pulled on her work gloves and headed out to the milking barn. She couldn't, after all, allow Peter to starve.

Could a zombie starve to death? Annie didn't know. After all, this plague of the undead had only started at the end of March, and while the newscasters had been clear that a good clean shot to the head would end a pesky zombie infestation, there was little information out yet on other methods of fixing one's zombie predicament. Not that she had any intention of letting Peter waste away— dead or undead, he was still indisputably the love of her life, and she intended to take care of him until a cure could be found.

Annie struggled with the rusty latch that held the screen door to the barn shut. She could hear Peter groaning inside, and smiled. He'd made it through the night's stifling heat just fine, and she greeted him with a singsong "Good *moor*-ning!" as she let herself into the milking parlor. Peter shook the chains around his neck and arms in response, emitting a low "mrrrrrr-rrr" in reply.

"It's me, darling. It's Annie! Can you say Annie? Come on Peter, say my name. An-nie?" She leaned her face in toward the bars that confined Peter, close enough to smell the rot of his skin but not so near that he could snake a bony claw through and get a grip on her. Peter moaned, turning away. He shuffled to the corner farthest away from her, fixing his blank gaze on the gray cement wall.

Annie was worried about Peter; she suspected he might be depressed. When she'd originally lured him into the barn and trapped him in one of the chutes built to hold the cows in place while they were being milked, he had been a frenzied, snarling mess. He'd howled and scrabbled at the clamp she'd swiftly fastened on his neck, foaming at the mouth. These days, he could barely muster up enough energy to dribble a little drool. She was sure it was because he was locked up in the damp, dank barn all day, every day. He probably missed the sunshine and fresh air.

Annie hummed as she started preparing for milking.

With Peter in one chute, this left only one side of the milking parlor open for the cows, and she had to carefully herd the girls toward the right side of the barn. She slid the back door open to find her final fourteen cows standing around, lowing softly, waiting for the relief of having their bags emptied. Her father had been milking these cows for a few years, and they knew the routine. The cows began to mosey into the parlor, lining themselves up with little direction from Annie. She squatted at the first station, and began the comforting rhythmic motions of milking.

The zombie plague had still been in its early stages when Peter was bitten. He'd gone to a party down at the reservoir alone that night, as Annie was still worn out from the effects of the Lyme disease she'd contracted earlier that April and had begged off from accompanying him. The antibiotics had sapped her of all energy—she hadn't even been helping her father out with the farm as much as she normally did, leaving Dad shorthanded. That night, her father was out late, feeding the calves, while Annie and her mother watched a History Channel program on the curse of the Kennedy family.

She and Peter had been dating for six months at that point, having met in the library of Manchester Community College, where they both went to school. She was studying to be a certified nursing assistant, and Peter was working toward his associate's in web design and development. She'd spotted him on one of the computers while she was studying at a table, and when he had looked up at her and winked, her mouth had dropped in surprise. Peter had immediately blushed and come over to apologize.

"I'm so sorry. I thought you were my sister. She's short

and has long brown hair, too."

"You wink at your sister often?"

"Yeah, why? Is that weird?"

"A little." Annie had shrugged, and the two had sat for a moment at the table, smiling goofily at each other. Peter had chocolate eyes and curly brown hair that hung just below his ears. He had a goatee that reminded her of Robert Downey Jr., which she didn't consider a bad thing at all. He'd asked her if she wanted to go out for a drink sometime, and she had accepted with a wide grin. They'd been dating ever since, and she had fallen schoolgirl-giddy in love, daydreaming about him in class and text messaging him while feeding the heifers their silage in the afternoons. He was charming and handsome and humble and totally into her, too, and Annie was smitten. They'd started having sex two months into the relationship, and for the first time in her twenty-two years of life, she had actually gotten emotional about sex. Being a farm girl, she'd been very matter-of-fact about the birds and the bees and the cows and the bulls, but Peter's ministrations had brought tears to her eyes.

"Let me just look at you," he'd whispered, stroking her hair after they'd made love on an old mattress in the back of his pickup truck. "You're so beautiful." Annie had grown up pitching hay and hauling grain, and she knew she was lean and limber. She had dark blue eyes and pin-straight hair that hung halfway down her back, and her most ambitious hairstyle was a ponytail. She'd always thought she looked wholesome at best, if not a little mannish. But Peter made her feel like a sex kitten. She loved that rush of power, knowing she could turn him on with just a glance. She had no intention of letting him go any time soon.

When Peter had shown up that night at her parents' house, she'd noticed something was off, but had chalked it up to too much beer at the party. He was slurring his words a little, and he couldn't seem to keep his eyes focused on her. He joined Annie and her mother in the living room to watch the terrible story of Mary Jo Kopechne unfold on the television, but his groaning quickly became distracting. It was then that Annie noticed the blood on Peter's collar, and the gaping wound on his neck.

"Oh my God! Peter, what happened?" He blinked at her stupidly, and Annie jumped up. "Let me get some gauze and antibiotic. Jeez, that looks bad—you might need stitches!" Annie hurried to the bathroom for Bactine and Band-Aids. It was when she returned to the living room and saw her boyfriend gnashing his teeth on her mother's skull that she'd realized something was very, very wrong with Peter.

"Mom!" she'd screamed, but it was too late. Her mother's eyes were glazed over, and Peter was scooping up her brains and gulping them down as if he hadn't tasted a more delectable sweetmeat in his life. Annie had been horrified. Somewhere in her mind she'd remembered that a craving for brains was one of the symptoms of the recent zombie epidemic, and this spurred her to action. She ran to her parent's bedroom and grabbed her father's pistol from his closet. She chambered a round and walked back slowly to the living room, taking careful aim.

It had been hard shooting her mother in the head, but

Annie knew that if she didn't, Mom would turn into a zombie herself. She couldn't let that happen to the funny, creative woman who had always made her daughter feel like she was a shining jewel. Mom deserved better.

Peter had looked up, startled when the head he was holding jolted between his hands. He snarled at her, and Annie was momentarily taken aback. Peter was supposed to love her. How *dare* he snarl at her!

Peter dropped the remains of Mom's head, wiped a piece of gray matter from his chin, and licked it off his finger. Then he pushed himself off the couch, slowly lumbering toward Annie. She turned on her heel and ran to the back door, which she burst out of, running squarely into her father's broad chest.

"Dad—run! It's Peter. He's a zombie!"

Her father grasped Annie by the arms, then caught sight of his best pistol, held tightly by the muzzle in Annie's right hand.

"Now, honey, I taught you better than that. You need to show a gun the respect it deserves when you're holding it. Here, like this." He swiftly took the gun and folded it against his chest as if he were nuzzling a soft kitten.

"Dad. It's Peter. He's a zombie. Mom's—well, Mom's gone."

"Mom's what?" Annie's father looked up, and then his gaze shifted to the blood-soaked undead figure lumbering toward them. "Is that Peter?"

"Dad, *run!*" Annie tried to tug on her father's arm to prompt him to move, but he shook her off. He slowly lifted the 38-caliber Ruger, carefully taking aim at his only precious daughter's zombified boyfriend. "Dad, no, stop!

It's still Peter!" She punched his right arm as hard as she could, throwing off her father's aim as Peter approached. Her father put a neat hole in the shingles that covered the side of their ranch house. Peter grabbed her father by the shoulders and bit into his face with a solid crunch. Annie heard her father's last screams as she sprinted to the barn.

When she'd initially escaped to the cowshed, it was to find a good hiding place to outwait Peter's cravings for cranial matter. But she soon realized, as she crept through the metal bars that kept the cows in place as they were milked, that what she had there was a tool she could use. A grade-A zombie cage, in fact. She'd gone into the barn office and found some heavy leg irons, ones her father and his herdsman used to hold the cows in place when the vet would come to inspect the Holsteins. She knew she had two advantages on her side—she was faster than Peter, and she could fit between the tapered bars of the milking chute. All she needed to do was lure him into the narrow, barred partition, get a few leg clamps on him, and she would have herself one angry, but neutralized, zombie.

Her plan had worked like a charm, and now she and Peter could wait this thing out, until a cure was found.

Annie glanced over at Peter as she milked. He was still facing the wall, moaning softly.

"Peter? You okay?" He let a slow glare slide her way, and moaned again.

Sometimes, Peter would react to her questions, or gaze at her with hunger in her eyes, and this was how Annie knew the man she loved was still inside the shell of this undead ghoul. His flesh was decaying, his hair was rotting out of his scalp, but deep down, he was still her Peter. She flashed him a bright smile and finished milking. She would worry about his depression later—right now, she had to feed the cows and pigs.

As Annie went about her routine, carrying bales of hay out to the trough, she wished she had real, *living* company. After trapping Peter, she'd wandered back to where her father lay, chopping off his head with the axe she'd found in the barn. It had been hard, nasty work, and she'd cringed with every blow. Then she'd dragged her father's torso out to the lagoon, where the cow's waste collected, and waded in. Knee deep in cow manure, she'd allowed her father's body to sink, slowly disappearing beneath the muck. Then she'd gone back for his head. Dad's eyes had popped open at the last second, and his mouth stretched into a grimace, right as Annie had launched his head into the lagoon, where it landed with a plop before sinking into the manure pit.

Annie could not allow herself to cry. To her, crying would be like giving in. She couldn't lose hope yet. Her parents were gone, killed by her brain-chomping, decaying boyfriend, but her heart kept telling her that one day Peter would be cured and they could put this terrible time behind them, living happily ever after. She had to believe this was true.

Annie made her way back to the house. It was lunchtime, and she made herself a grilled cheese and a cup of hot tomato soup. She turned on the television to catch the twelve o'clock news. There were riots in the streets of New York City, and Times Square was being overrun by zombies. The National Guard had been called in, and the camera panned out to several young men in full riot gear taking aim at the shambling undead. Heads exploded on the screen as the camera zoomed in on the crowd. The newscaster, a young brunette woman in a black suit and too much makeup, looked flustered. Annie noticed the microphone in the woman's hand shook slightly as she turned the show back over to the anchors in the newsroom.

Annie missed interacting with the living, but there didn't seem to be anyone left on their rural country road. She'd thought about going into town to see what was happening and who was left, but Annie was scared. The television broadcast images of putrefying zombies lumbering through the streets of towns all across the country; Annie herself had seen more undead than survivors just looking out the window. Two or three reanimated corpses would drag themselves down the road each day. The closest neighbor, Annie's old high school French teacher, had wandered past about a week ago. Annie had adored Madame Bestow, and almost called out to her when she saw the familiar figure walk by with her wiry gray hair tightly wound in a bun, wearing a cardigan, skirt and sensible flats, but Annie'd hesitated. Madame's bun seemed straggly; a few wisps of hair were out of place and flying wild. Her skirt was ripped on the side, and her leg had what appeared to be a large, festering gash in her calf. Something was not quite right with Madame Bestow. Annie'd put her hand to her mouth, afraid to move or make a noise. Madame shuffled along past the house, toward town, and Annie breathed a sigh of relief once she was out of sight.

Annie didn't have high hopes that she would find many

living people left. She turned her mind to the task of cheering Peter up. Maybe a field trip outside of the cage was in order.

There was a major downside to this, of course. To solve the problem of getting Peter out of the barn without attacking her, she could only think of one solution: she was going to have to put a cold steel ring through his nose, much like a farmer leading a bull. There seemed to be no other way, and Annie dreaded the task of installing the ring itself. She'd found a box of bull rings in the barn office, as well as a hook to help lead him around, but nothing to help numb the pain. Whether Peter felt pain or not was still undetermined, but if he could get the blues, she suspected there were still enough synapses firing to make him wince when she punctured his nose. And getting the ring through his septum was going to be tough: she'd debated using a paper-hole punch, but decided that was *too* cruel. She was going to have to restrain him and manually push the metal through, just like she'd done to herself when she'd pierced her own ears. She still remembered how much that had hurt. She shuddered to think how Peter would react.

She decided to go back out to the barn and visit with him, to see how he felt about the idea. Annie strongly believed that sometimes, with his series of grunts and moans, Peter was desperately trying to communicate with her. She would run the notion of a field trip by him and get his grunts on the matter.

Peter was sitting cross-legged on the cement floor, rocking slowly back and forth. Annie's eyes welled with tears to see him reduced to such a state. Blood crusted his filthy, grimy clothes, and maggots squirmed in a hole in his cheek that was widening by the day. He was falling apart, and Annie could do nothing to stop it. She struggled to remember the gentle young man who had traced soft patterns on her arm, caressing her as they spoke of their dream jobs, the type of home they'd like to live in (they'd both agreed that an in-ground pool would be heavenly), even possible names for their future children. Her heart skipped a beat as she remembered his touch. She was so—*well, let's face it*, she thought. *You're so horny it hurts.*

She swallowed hard and let out a short bark of a laugh at her predicament. Peter looked up and attempted to smile. Annie *thought* it was a smile, anyway. The flesh around his lips had rotted away, so it was more of a gaping maw through which his teeth and gums loomed large. Annie's heart soared at the sight of it, though. *He recognizes me,* she thought. *He remembers that he loves me.*

"Peter? Honey? How you doing in there?" Peter continued to stare at her, and she prattled on. "How would you feel about going outside? Get some sun, maybe?"

Peter unfolded his legs, standing quickly, and his speed alarmed Annie. She hadn't thought he could move so fast. She supposed, though, with the proper motivation, even the decaying undead could show flashes of swiftness. Like chickens, who mostly walked and pecked at the ground, but took flight in bursts of flurried feathers when alarmed. She continued.

"Here's the thing, though. I don't know that you won't try to eat me as soon as I let you out, so, ah, I have to take steps." Peter tilted his head slightly. A long line of spittle stretched down off his chin, reaching toward the ground.

"I'd like to . . . well, I'd like to give you a nose ring. How do you feel about that?"

Peter blinked again, but gave no indication that he understood. He wasn't grunting or moaning, though, which Annie took as a good sign. She held up the ring. The cold steel circle looked black in the dim light of the barn, and Peter's eyes shifted to the loop in her hand. His forehead creased, but he didn't turn away. Annie moved closer, and started unhurriedly pulling tauter the chains that attached to the clamps on his arms and legs.

"I just have to make sure you're restrained, darling," she jabbered on, tightening his bonds. "I've seen some bulls go crazy during this procedure, and that's even after the vet shoots their nose with Novocain. I know it'll hurt," she said, as Peter began to tug back, resisting the constriction of his chains. "But it'll all be worth it in the end, right?"

Peter was stretched wide now, his arms and legs fanned out in an X with his back against the steel bars. He yowled at his predicament, struggling to pull free. Annie slipped between the bars and gently touched his face.

"I love you," she whispered, and unclamped the ring.

Annie struggled to stab the ring through the soft flesh of his septum, and Peter howled in pain and rage as she pushed. The ring was making a deeper puncture wound than she'd anticipated, and she was having a hard time getting it to poke through the skin. Peter began to yelp— loud, agony-filled wails—and Annie squared her shoulders and tried again. This time, the ring broke through the sensitive tissue, and she was able to clamp it shut. She was breathing heavily, and realized she'd been clenching her teeth. She stretched out her jaw, opening her mouth wide, hearing it crack near her ears. "That was tougher than I thought it'd be," she laughed, looking at Peter. His eyes were squeezed tightly shut. His yelps had been reduced to a low keening, and for a moment, Annie felt guilty. She'd just mangled him, after all. Dead or undead, it had to hurt.

"We'll go out in a little while," she murmured in his ear, before squeezing through the bars to loosen his chains. "In the meantime, I'll bring you a nice pig."

Peter ripped open the pig's skull with less enthusiasm than normal, Annie noted. There were tracks in the grime on his face, and she realized he'd been crying. She hated to see him like this, but she was at a loss for what else to do. It was all for his own good. She decided to wait a couple of days before bringing him outside, to let his nose heal a little bit. She didn't want to ruin his big day out by tugging at the ring and causing him pain every time.

When Peter finished cleaning out the pig's brain from its cranial cavity, he leaned back against the wall, giving the boar's corpse a little kick. He closed his eyes. Annie could see his eyes moving back and forth beneath his lids. She leaned in to tug at the pig's hoof, trying to maneuver the corpse down to the other end of the chute, where she could pull it out of Peter's cage and pile it with the other animal bodies just outside the barn door. She'd been using a sort of winch that she'd crafted with ropes and a hook to move the cows' corpses once Peter had fed on them, but she'd been unable to pull them very far, even with the pulley. The smell of the dead animals was unbearable, and Annie invariably vomited every day when she had to move a fresh body to the pile. She had taken to swiping Vick's

Vapo-Rub under her nose before this task, but the nauseating stench still made her eyes water. It was her least favorite part of the day, and she tried to get it over with as quickly as possible.

Annie had to open a metal gate to pull the corpse through, and Peter often made a stab at escaping when he heard her rattle the chain to unlock it. She kept her father's pistol tucked in to the waistband of her shorts, and had had to fire more than one warning shot in Peter's general direction. Today, however, he made no move to escape, and Annie figured his nose was probably still throbbing. She cleaned up the pig remains, hosed Peter's cell down, and closed the barn door. Another beautiful day spent in the company of the zombie she loved.

Peter seemed excited when Annie pulled out the hook a few days later, and she was encouraged that he recognized that the gaff meant he was going outside. If he could still reason out this association, she figured, then some part of him was still Peter, the man, not all Peter, the cannibalistic monster. He winced as she hooked his nose ring through the bar, but waited patiently, moaning faintly from the back of his throat, as she unhooked the clamps holding his neck, arms, and legs. Slowly she led him outside, through the barn door. Peter walked with timid steps, and held up his arm, gurgling, when the sunlight hit his face. Annie giggled. For the first time in ages, Peter seemed happy.

She led him out to the meadow next to the barn. She'd been worried about ticks, and sprayed herself with Deep Woods Off—she certainly didn't want to deal with Lyme disease again, not after the summer she'd been having—

but decided Peter would probably be okay. His skin was a mottled gray, with blackish-purple sores sprinkled across his arms and legs, and she figured the ticks would almost certainly leave him alone. She watched him, heart soaring, as Peter's mouth widened. A barn cat joined them in the field, and rubbed against the tattered remains of Peter's Levis. He grunted, seeming to delight in the feline's attentions. Peter leaned over and scooped the cat up into his festering claws. He sank his teeth into the cat's muzzle with one quick chomp.

Annie gave a sharp tug at the nose ring with the gaff to get him to release the poor animal, and watched in horror as the ring ripped through the rotting flesh of his nose, falling off the end of the hook onto the grass with a *plunk*. Peter continued to gnaw on the cat's head, sucking brains out through the holes where the cat's eyes had been a moment before. Annie let out a shriek in spite of herself, and Peter jerked his head up, raising his eyebrows. He spotted the ring on the ground, and this time, Annie was sure: he was *smiling*, a wide, toothy, hideous grin. She pulled the pistol out of her waistband, flipped off the safety, and took aim.

"Peter." She sighed. "I don't want to do this, honey. Please just shuffle your way into the barn, and we can get back to our normal routine."

Peter straightened, dropping the corpse and brushing cat hair off of his threadbare jeans. He continued to leer, and took a hesitant step toward her. "Please don't," Annie begged. "I don't want to hurt you. I love you so much; please don't make me blow your head off."

"Ahh-naaaa," Peter groaned.

Annie let the gun drop to her side, stunned.

"Did you—did you just say my name?" she whispered.

"Ahh-naa!" Peter repeated, edging closer, holding out his arms to her. "Ahh-naa!" He stopped, cocked his head, and winked.

Tears streamed down Annie's face as she stepped into his arms. Peter was back; he still loved her, and everything was going to be okay. Her soulmate had returned to her, and—ugh. She recoiled a little in spite of herself. The smell of decomposing flesh was repulsive, and her stomach lurched. She struggled to pull away, but Peter just held on tighter as she squirmed.

Annie started to screech, a high-pitched, guttural wail, but the scream died in her throat. It was drowned out by the cracking of her skull as Peter bit down to feed.

INTERLUDE: A TALE THAT FAILED

A message from the author:
I'm sorry to report that not every short story is a walk in the park to write. Sometimes, you have those days where it's a struggle to get the words out onto the paper. Enter my mind, if you will, for just a moment, and you will see why "Blossom vs. the Zombie Werewolves" was, sadly, never meant to be.

Me typing:
Blossom sat on the red tiles of the kitchen floor, watching as her mother pulled pumpkin spice muffins out of the oven.

Wait a minute. This is my story, and I hate pumpkin.

Blossom sat on the red tiles of the kitchen floor, watching as her mother pulled chocolate chip muffins out of the oven.

Much better.

I sure am hungry.

Blossom's mother, Violette, had been married to Harold Rock for sixteen years.

Wait—now I remember why I liked the name Blossom Rock for a character so much. That's the actress who played Grandmamma on *The Addams Family*. Crap.

Blossom's mother, Violette, had been married to Harold Cohen for sixteen years.

I had a roommate in college with the last name Cohen. Since my plan for Violette involves dismemberment by zombie, my old roommate could sue me for wrongful death via literary character. Could get messy.

Blossom's mother, Violette, had been married to Harold Jones for sixteen years.

Am I supposed to write out sixteen? Can't I just use the number 16? Where is my proofreading bible?

Found it. Looks like the cat barfed on it, and now the pages are all stuck together. I'll have to figure out some other literary fix for this.

Blossom's mother, Violette Jones, had never married Blossom's father, a struggling artist named Flea whom she had picked up hitchhiking one day. After a night of passion among the desert cacti, she had left him outside of Phoenix, never to see him again.

Much better. . . . Except wasn't Flea the name of that guitarist from Red Hot Chili Peppers? And I was worried about my *roommate* suing me?

. . . a struggling artist named Roach whom she had picked up hitchhiking one day.

Do I have any chocolate chip muffin mix? I sure could go for something sweet right now. Wait a minute. I think there's an old Ring Ding in the junk food drawer.

Score!

Violette was late for her Weight Watchers meeting.

I suppose an apple and a cup of green tea *would* be more sensible.

Violette crouched down to where Blossom was sitting cross-legged on the floor. "Blossom, honey? Will you be okay by yourself for a little while so that Momma can go learn how to be skinny?"

Jeez, what kind of mother leaves her four-year-old home alone? I'm glad she's getting disemboweled.

Blossom sucked her fingers in reply. Outside, the wolves were howling.

Uh-oh. THAT can't be good.

Blossom stood by the front door, watching as her mother's taillights receded into the darkness. Suddenly, a slobbering monstrosity of a wolf, with wild gray hair and burning red eyes, jumped onto the front stoop. It snarled, spittle and blood dripping from its fangs. Blossom jumped back from the screen door, then smiled.

"Good doggy," she lisped, opening the door.

Well, so much for Blossom. This is exactly why I'm a cat person.

So you see? Sometimes a story just doesn't want to work itself out. Clearly, the only sensible thing to do at this point is to drive to Dunkin' Donuts and work out the story's problems over a chocolate chip muffin.

I apologize for this interruption. You may now resume reading the short stories that *did*, thankfully, work themselves out.

TRAPPED

Ed and Dawn Bloom had been together for thirty-five years. If asked, they both would've admitted that while the passion and excitement had long left their marriage, for the most part they were content with the life they'd made together. They fully expected to continue on in their familiar pattern, hand in hand, until death did them part, with few moments of real joy or happiness, but little disappointment, either.

That was before the snow came.

***

They'd met at the construction company where Ed was a drywaller and Dawn kept the books. She'd been twenty-five at the time, Ed a year older, and she'd found his warm blue eyes appealing, his sinewy frame a sight to be appreciated. He'd been intimidated by her college degree and her standoffish nature with the crews, but he couldn't help admiring her brunette waves and the way her lips would purse into a bright red pout whenever one of the guys would tell an off-color joke. It had taken a year for Ed to work up the courage to ask her out, and another six months, after the construction company went under and Ed had applied to Connecticut College for lack of something better to do, before Dawn would accept. They'd shared a love of books and jigsaw puzzles, and she'd helped him study and budget for his college courses, until he finally graduated with a degree in business administration. They were married two weeks after graduation, and had bought a three-bedroom Colonial in Amston, a tiny town ideal for raising their two sons when they came along. Ed started up a hardware store down the road from Ted's Market and Dawn was his bookkeeper, helping out at the shop on the weekends so Ed could spend time coaching the boys' soccer teams and leading their scout troops. Every Sunday, Ed and Dawn would do the *New York Times* crossword puzzle together at the kitchen table over coffee.

The boys, Jimmy and Marty, were grown and gone. Jimmy had followed in his father's footsteps, studying business management and starting up his own hardware distribution company. He'd settled in Florida, where the low corporate and unemployment taxes, coupled with the sunny weather, had proven too enticing for Jimmy to pass up. He'd married a nice girl from Pensacola, and they had a daughter, Jenny. Framed pictures of their granddaughter lined the wall of the stairs leading up to the second floor of Ed and Dawn's house, and Ed often announced that his biggest regret was that they didn't get to see Jenny more than a couple of times a year.

Dawn's biggest regret was that her youngest son,

Marty, clearly showed signs of never growing up, despite having turned thirty this past year. His latest adventure had taken him to Los Angeles, where he'd followed his girlfriend in hopes of starting a career writing movie scripts. That Marty had barely passed his high school composition class did not seem to faze him, and Dawn spent many nights worrying about how he was living and paying his bills. She'd decided just last night to send him some money and a care package when Ed went into the shop for the day. Ed would turn three shades of purple if he knew of her plans to help their shiftless son yet again, but she had a small account of her own that she'd been building up over the years, started for emergencies just such as this, that Ed didn't know about. She'd write the check out of there, and Ed would be none the wiser. She'd woken up that morning anxious for Ed to leave so she could get started on her box of goodies for Marty.

"Looks like the weatherman got it wrong yet again," Ed said when she shuffled into the kitchen. Ed delighted in the incompetency of the local meteorologist, Roland van Berg, and each forecast that was wrong had a tendency to put Ed in an almost giddy mood. "Look at that snow coming down outside. Light dusting, my fanny."

Dawn peeked out the window over the sink and sighed. Small, heavy flakes of white were falling steadily, and from her best estimation, six inches already coated the ground. If it didn't let up soon, Ed would stay home for the day, and she would have to spend another sleepless night worrying about her son all the way on the other side of the country, probably not able to afford peanut butter or soap.

"Should let up soon, though, shouldn't it?" she asked,

trying to keep the frustration out of her voice. "I mean, he couldn't have mixed up a light dusting with a blizzard, right?" She smoothed her hand over her short salt-and-pepper cap of hair, wondering if she should bother to brush it if she wasn't going to get out of the house after all. She poured herself a cup of coffee, waiting for Ed to respond.

"Doesn't look like it's going to slow down anytime soon to me. Roland Van Berg is a numbskull. I'll have to get out there and shovel soon," Ed grumbled, as if the weatherman himself was to blame for this act of labor. "How about some eggs?" he asked, brightening, and Dawn nodded, reaching for the frying pan.

Over the years, Ed had helped out many of the locals with their home improvement projects after they stopped by his store for supplies. As a result, he was still lean and muscled at sixty-one, and Dawn was certain he could clear their front walkway with little effort. His hair had gone gray and thinned considerably, but when he flashed his dimples in a broad smile, she would catch a glimpse of the young, eager man with whom she'd first fallen in love. His cholesterol was high, due to a weakness for peppermint stick ice cream, but otherwise, his health was good. She felt a twinge of jealousy over this when she let herself think about it. Dawn herself struggled with arthritis and high blood pressure. She was carrying about fifty pounds of extra weight, which didn't help either medical condition, and her knees creaked early in the morning. Not that Ed had ever complained—if anything, he was more complimentary than ever in regards to her ample bosom—but her wide hips and neck wattle bothered her. Ruth

Miller from her book club had been talking about going to a Weight Watchers meeting in town one of these days, and Dawn was considering going with her. Eggs sounded like a light, healthy meal, so Dawn got out the milk, bread for toast, and set about cooking breakfast.

After they ate in silence, Dawn started cleaning up the dishes and wiping down the kitchen counter while Ed went into the entryway to pull on his boots and gloves. She was humming, thinking about Marty, and the thumping from the hallway didn't register at first. It happened a few more times before Dawn rinsed off the frying pan and turned off the water.

"Ed? You okay?"

"No, I'm not okay! I can't get the gull darn door open!"

Dawn wiped her hands on the dishtowel and poked her head around the corner to see what he was talking about.

"Is it broken again?" They'd had problems in the past with the spring on the storm door popping off; Ed had replaced it three or four times already, but couldn't seem to get it to take.

"No, it's not the stupid spring. It's the stupid snow! It's blocking the door!"

"Doesn't look like that much out the window," Dawn offered, moving closer. "What if we both push on it?"

"What if we both push on it?" he mimicked in a high-pitched voice. "Jeez, Dawn, if *I* can't get it open, what on earth makes you think you can? You can't even open a jar of peanut butter without my help, and the darn thing's a screw top." He glared at his wife, who was pursing her pretty rose lips in a scowl.

"Do it yourself then," she spat, stung by his words. She

threw down the dish towel and stalked off to what had once been Marty's room, but which now held their computer and home office. If he was going to get testy with her, well, she'd hole up in the office for a while. He could shovel the walk by himself.

Dawn turned on the computer and waited for it to warm up. It was an old Gateway, and she'd hinted to Ed for a few months leading up to the holiday that she'd like a new one for Christmas. Ed had apparently missed all the clues she'd dropped, and had given her a paper shredder instead. She frowned at the new appliance now, collecting dust in the corner of the room. His argument had been that since they could only get dial-up in their area, a new computer wouldn't be any faster than the old clunker they had now. A paper shredder only required an electrical outlet to shred credit card applications and insurance quote offers, all with dual cross-cutting action.

"Dear Lord," she murmured, "let him get that walkway clear before I go crazy and kill that man." She double-clicked on the Internet icon to read her e-mail and see what the Weather Channel website was predicting about the storm.

Dawn was staring at a Doppler map, mouth agape, when Ed found her in the office. He'd taken off his boots, but snow still clung to the legs of his pants.

"I managed to get out there and get the stoop clear, but that's a real heavy snow coming down," he started, brushing off the flakes from his trousers. "Seems pointless for me to do the whole path while it's still snowing. Sorry I snapped at you earlier," he added, and walked behind the chair where his wife was sitting, putting a hand on her shoulder.

"Hush up and look at this," Dawn stuttered. "Look at the size of this storm!"

The computer screen showed a large blue-gray mass slowly swirling above most of New England. "It's supposed to keep coming down all day! I can't believe we had no warning—your weatherman is a total ninny!" She blew out a breath of air loudly; harshly.

"Calm down now, woman. It's just snow. It's not like we've never seen the white stuff before, for goodness sake. We'll just sit tight until it's over and dig ourselves out, same as everybody else."

"How are we going to plow out if you can't even shovel the front walk? You going to call up Bob down the road and ask him to help us out?"

Dawn and Ed shared a long driveway with one other house, owned by Bob Deveraux. The houses were just over a half mile apart, but the neighbors had had a tumultuous relationship since Bob moved in twenty years ago. Dawn and Ed had gone over with a plate of muffins shortly after Bob bought the house. Bob had answered the door drunk as a skunk at eleven o'clock in the morning. He'd insisted on showing them around the property; Ed had spotted log-splitting equipment in the woods on their tour. The wood-filled trucks Ed sometimes encountered in the driveway when coming home had confirmed his suspicions, and he'd called town hall to report that Bob was illegally operating a commercial business in a residential zone. The building official had been happy to tell Bob exactly who'd ratted him out when he shut down his business, and the neighbors had been at war ever since.

Over the years, Bob had spilled nails in the driveway, called child services on the Blooms regularly when the boys were young, stole their newspapers, and bought chickens, feeding them every night by spreading cornmeal in the driveway right around the time Ed usually came home. Ed and Dawn had fought back. They'd called the game warden every time they caught a glimpse of Bob heading out in camouflage before deer season started, poured salt down his well, and adopted a pit bull to go after the chickens. The dog, Killer, had disappeared some years ago, and the Blooms had called the police to report that they'd heard a gunshot near Bob's house right around the time Killer had gone missing. The local sheriff, tired of the feuding, had politely ignored the situation with the hope that it would quietly go away. Bob hadn't replaced the chickens that Killer had eaten, and the Blooms had not bothered to replace Killer, so on this one point, the sheriff had gotten his wish. But there was still no love lost between the two houses, and Ed needed to clear *out* the driveway before Bob tried to plow them *in*.

"That miserable coot isn't going to be any more successful at clearing out the snow than we are," Ed said with conviction, and patted his wife's shoulder again. "Come on now, hon. Let's make some hot chocolate and watch old Gary Cooper movies."

Dawn was not about to turn down a screening of *Mr. Deeds Goes to Town,* so she put the computer to sleep and followed her husband to the living room.

They managed to make it an hour into the movie before the bickering started again. "God, her voice is annoying," Ed said when Jean Arthur appeared for the umpteenth time to flirt with Coop.

"It's part of her charm." Dawn scooped up another handful of popcorn.

"I hardly think Jean Arthur got movie roles because of her voice," Ed replied, moving his hands to simulate a curvy figure.

"They wouldn't have kept hiring her if she couldn't act," Dawn pointed out, but Ed dismissed her with a wave.

"They would if she were putting out on the casting couch." Ed chuckled, a rough giggle that made Dawn's fillings ache.

"Oh, shut up. You have no idea if Jean Arthur put out or not." Dawn crossed her arms over her chest and tried hard to listen to the unfolding courtroom scene.

"I'm just sayin'," Ed's voice rose, "she's no great shakes as an actress and her voice is annoying. A girl like that would've had to use her looks and her bod to break into the business."

Enough. "I'm going upstairs to read for a while before Jean Arthur causes our divorce," Dawn announced, standing. *Thanks for ruining one of my favorite movies,* she added in her head, and stomped up the stairs.

Dawn crawled on top of the covers and flipped open the book she was reading, a mystery by Rita Mae Brown. She found she was too irritated to read, though, and slammed the book shut in frustration after a few minutes. *Okay, girl, why are you so mad?* she thought, trying to work out her aggravation.

Because I didn't know it was going to snow. Because I can't get a package out to my son, and I'm worried about him. Because I'm stuck in the house with a man who prefers to speculate on Jean

Arthur's casting couch antics instead of shutting the hell up and watching the movie.

Because I feel trapped.

That was it, really. She felt trapped in the house with Ed. They'd lived together for thirty-five years with independent schedules and lives, and rarely spent more than a few hours at a stretch in each other's company. With the exception of family vacations, which they hadn't gone on in years, they weren't used to spending the whole day together, with nothing to do.

Dawn sighed and headed back down the stairs. "I'm sorry. The snow's gotten my nerves frayed," she started apologizing, and looked at Ed, still on the couch. A soft snore emitted from his lips. While she had been practically pulling her hair out, worrying about their marriage, he'd decided to take a nap.

I hate him, she thought, and went in to the kitchen to bake cookies.

Kneading the cookie dough helped calm her nerves. Dawn set her mind to preparing for the worst, in case the storm didn't let up for a while. She filled the bathtub with water, and put fresh batteries in the flashlights. She was taking another shot at reading while her cookies cooled when she heard Ed stirring on the couch. He was shuffling into the bathroom when the microwave beeped and the lights blinked out.

"Oh, crap," Ed muttered, the tiles in the bathroom adding an echo to his words. "Better bring up some wood from the basement." The house had electric heat, but there was a fireplace in the living room, which did a decent job of heating the main floor, if not the upstairs. "I guess we can pull out the couch and sleep down here tonight if the power doesn't come back on." Ed came into the kitchen and looked out at the blanket of white that was still coming down. He didn't sound particularly happy about the prospect, so Dawn stood up and wrapped her arms around his waist.

"That sounds romantic," she cooed. "We can have fondue and cookies for dinner . . . maybe a little wine?"

"Wine and cookies?" Ed turned around in Dawn's embrace and made a face. He kissed her quickly on the lips. "Feeling better now?"

"Better now." She nodded.

"Done defending Jean Arthur's virtue?" He smiled, and she stuck out her tongue.

"Don't you start," she said, wagging her finger at him, and he let a hand graze down to her waist before turning to the basement door.

"Better grab that wood before the pipes freeze." He sighed, letting an appreciating gaze linger on her hips.

Dawn fished out some old candles from the junk drawer, and pulled out the hide-away bed in the living room. She put fresh sheets on the mattress and went upstairs to grab the pillows off of their bed. Her knees grumbled as she climbed; she really had to get to that Weight Watchers meeting with Ruth. She looked around the bedroom and frowned. She'd been planning on doing a little vacuuming while the snow fell; now that the power was out, she didn't know what to do with herself.

"Any idea when this is supposed to let up?" she shouted down the stairs.

"How the hell should I know?" Ed barked. "I get my

weather report from that genius, Roland van Berg, remember?" Dawn dug her nails into her palms and said nothing. *I'm sure he's just stir crazy too*, she reasoned, but it did little to smooth her ruffled feathers. Ed came up from the basement, breathing heavily with his arms full of wood, as Dawn was descending from the bedroom. She curled up on the flat couch mattress and returned to her novel while Ed worked on lighting a fire.

Dawn finished her book and managed to wipe down all the windows and sills on the main floor before night fell. Once the fire had caught and swelled to a comfortable glow, Ed had returned outside to the stoop to shovel some more. He came in at dusk, cold emanating off of his clothes and body.

"Take off those wet things and I'll start pulling dinner together," she offered, and Ed winked.

"You just want to get me naked," he purred, and started to peel off the layers.

"How is it out there?"

"Still doesn't look like it's going to stop any time soon," Ed admitted, shaking the snow out of his hair. "Hope it stops by the morning. If it keeps coming down like this, we're going to have to figure out a way to knock some of the snow off the roof."

Dawn rummaged through the kitchen by candlelight. She pulled out the fondue set and asked Ed to grab the cans of Sterno off the shelves in the basement. She cubed a loaf of day-old Italian bread she'd bought on a whim yesterday. She'd planned on making cauliflower cheese soup this week, and was grateful for both the fresh cauliflower and the bars of Velveeta she'd picked up in anticipation. They'd have a nice meal tonight despite the circumstances. Lord only knew what tomorrow would bring, but they'd make it through the evening just fine.

They ate dinner in the living room by the light of the fireplace, dipping cauliflower and bread into melted Velveeta fondue. They undressed for bed and made love lazily. Ed sighed.

"Now what?" he joked, and she smiled. They normally wouldn't go to bed for at least a couple more hours, but there wasn't much to do except read and pace the house.

"Hey," she offered with a shrug, "I was the one who wanted to buy a generator." It was a discussion that came up every so often, but Ed always dismissed the idea as too expensive and time consuming. Dawn had argued that the cost and maintenance would be worth it. The power went out at least three or four times a year, and they'd lost more than one refrigerator full of food.

"Don't start, Dawn." Ed frowned, sitting up.

"I'm just conversationally pointing out that it sure would've been helpful tonight if we'd had one," Dawn said, reaching over to take Ed's hand. He pulled away from her grasp.

"I don't think you understand what the situation's really like outside," he said, choosing his words carefully. "Even if we had a generator out back, I wouldn't be able to get near it. We probably have twenty inches out there right now."

"So we put it close to the house," Dawn countered, and Ed held his hand up, palm out, cutting her off.

"Wouldn't matter. Besides the carbon monoxide issue, I can't even shovel down to the *driveway*, Dawn. A generator would be no good to us right now."

"Ed Bloom, you are the most stubborn man I've ever met. The only reason we don't have a generator is because Bob Deveraux has one and you'd rather rip off your own arm and beat yourself with it than admit that that man actually had a good idea." She stood up quickly, gathering the dinner dishes, rattling them loudly.

"*I'm* stubborn?" Ed started, but she stalked off to the kitchen before he could finish. Dawn dropped the dishes in the sink with a clatter. *Let them break*, she thought, clenching her teeth. *With all the money we saved on not buying a generator, we can buy a whole new set of dishes. That'll keep us warm in the winter.*

She heard Ed slam the door to the bathroom. He did remember that the toilet wouldn't fill with the power out, didn't he? She fished out the Sterno pots from the pile of plates and wiped them off with a dishrag.

Heading to the basement stairs, she paused for a moment outside the bathroom door to see if Ed would realize the toilet tank would have to be filled manually to flush. He swung the door open with no telltale *woosh* of the toiled preceding him, and hesitated when he saw her at the top of the basement stairs.

"What?"

"Did you just poop?" Dawn asked. "I refuse to smell that all night. What do you plan on doing about it?" Somewhere inside her mind, a tiny voice said *you might be overreacting, Dawn, just a hair, when you gotta go, you gotta go, snowstorm or not,* but she'd had it. She couldn't stand to be around her husband for one more minute.

"Jeez, relax! You're being a real bitch tonight, you

know that? I'm gonna get the dehumidifier bucket out of the basement and fill the tank with the water from that. Calm down!" Ed pushed past her on the stairs just as Dawn turned to walk down, and she was thrown off balance. Her foot stepped out, only to meet empty space. The Sterno cans flew as she rolled down the steps, banging her head and shoulders against the banister bars as she fell. Just as she slammed facedown on the rug at the bottom, she felt her knee twist in a hot flash of pain. Dawn couldn't help herself. She screamed.

"Oh my God, Dawn! Are you okay? I didn't mean it, oh my God, I'm so sorry." Ed's words jumbled over themselves as he hurried to her. She stopped screaming and started breathing hard, like she was taught to do in the Lamaze classes she took before Jimmy was born. She didn't think she could bear the agonizing waves that were strangling her knee. Flashes of color pinpricked her vision.

Please let me pass out, God. Just for a little while.

Ed continued to blubber. He sat on the floor beside her, raised her head and put it in his lap, so she was now blinking at his crotch. "It's okay, honey; you'll be fine. We're gonna be okay. Can you stand? Are you bleeding?" Dawn lifted her head and turned to see if her kneecap was now on the underside of her knee. Her right leg sprawled out alongside her, bent at an awkward angle. Ed continued. "Jesus. I'm so sorry. It was an accident. Are you okay, honey?" Her knee was already swelling, and she looked up at her husband's face. The tears streaming down her cheeks matched his. *I hate you,* she thought, looking into his eyes, and he flinched. She gulped. Had she actually said that out loud? No, she couldn't have. She was still doing her Lamaze breathing. But Ed had received the message just the same.

Ed helped her to her feet, but she cried out when she tried to put weight on the right leg. She couldn't walk. "Is it broken?" Ed asked meekly, and she glared at him. She wanted, more than anything, to slap him. And to walk. To be able to walk and slap him, yes, these two things alone would make her happy. The pain still came in waves and she became conscious of the grinding noise she was making with her teeth.

"I think"—she breathed out slowly, working through another wave—"I need to go to the hospital. In fact, I'm pretty damn sure of it."

Ed looked miserable. "I can call 911, but they won't be able to make it up the driveway, much less drive you into Manchester," he lamented. She leaned in close to him, jaw still locked.

"Call them *anyway*," she hissed through her teeth. He sat Dawn on the bottom basement step and retrieved the cell phone from her purse, quickly returning to her side.

Ed had been right. The ambulance would not be able to get to them, Dawn heard the dispatcher tell Ed apologetically. It was Linda Orr, the sweet young redhead who used to babysit the boys from time to time, and so was familiar with the Blooms' long, winding driveway. She talked Ed through what he should do, advising him to make sure Dawn kept ice on her knee and her leg elevated.

"And I'd get her here as soon as the snow stops, Mr. Bloom. It sounds like she may have torn a few ligaments at the very least, and she's gonna need some pain medication and an X-ray. Do you have any whiskey?"

"Are you advising me to get my wife drunk, Linda?" Ed asked. Dawn shook her head next to him, wincing.

"I sure am, Mr. Bloom. It's gonna be a long storm."

Ed helped Dawn back up the stairs. She managed to hop to the couch, arms wrapped around his neck, Ed bearing the brunt of her weight. Once she was on the pull-out bed, she was able to get a better look at the damage. From her knee down to her ankle, the skin was puffed and bruising already. She sat, twisted leg stretched out in front of her, and wept quietly. Ed disappeared for a moment, returning with the dusty bottle of scotch they kept on hand for guests.

"Have some. It'll help," he said, pouring her a shot.

"I can't get drunk. It'll make me have to pee, and we don't have power to flush the toilet," Dawn said, and she could hear the whine in her own voice. "Plus, I can't get up and down that much."

"I'll go get that bucket and put it by the bed." Ed sighed, and Dawn unscrewed the scotch bottle. The raw stabs of pain were unbearable and unrelenting. She knocked back her first shot.

A funny thing happened as Dawn started to feel a pleasant buzz from the alcohol. The more she drank, the more Dawn found she appreciated her husband. He had provided for her and her sons admirably, not just with the store but with his presence. He'd taught the boys how to swim at Amston Lake and Dawn how to install a new battery in her car. He was providing for her now, crawling into the attic with a flashlight to find the crutches Marty had used when he broke his foot sliding into home base in seventh grade. She'd suspected years ago that her husband had been attracted to Linda the babysitter, watching as his eyes sometimes followed her walk a little too long, but sure he'd never acted on it. Women flirted with him every day at the shop, but as far as Dawn could tell, he was oblivious to their overtures. He was a good man.

"I love you," she slurred when he returned to her, cobwebbed crutches in hand.

"I love you too, honey. I think you might be boozing it up a little too much. You sound like Dudley Moore in *Arthur*." She giggled, and then cried out when she accidentally jostled her own leg. "I'm going to see if I can't find something to splint that up," he explained, and retreated to the basement again.

When Dawn awoke the next morning, her leg was braced by two planks of wood, secured with duct tape. Ed had dressed her in thin cotton pajama bottoms first, so the duct tape wouldn't stick against her skin. She tried to swing her legs over the side of the bed. A stab of agony cut through her splinted knee, and she had to slowly scoot forward to get the heel of her leg to touch the floor.

"How am I supposed to move around?" she griped, then moaned. Her head was tapping out a steady pounding samba beat, and she reached for the bucket to throw up. Her retching caused her husband to stir beside her.

"I put the aspirin and a glass of water next to you," he yawned, and she nodded weakly in thanks. Her head and knee thrummed, and she was afraid that the strain of vomiting would cause her to wet the bed.

"Help me up," she whimpered, and Ed was by her side, pulling her up by the elbow.

The crutches were too tall, and she wriggled impatiently

while Ed adjusted them to her height. She teetered over to the bathroom, slowly lowering herself down on the toilet. "Don't look," she shouted out to her husband. "I can't shut the door." In thirty-five years of marriage, they'd never once left the bathroom door open when they'd used it, and she was ashamed to start now. Dawn peed, and her stomach lurched again. She dry-heaved onto the bathroom floor, crying. She couldn't remember being more humiliated in her life. "I need a towel," she called out to Ed. "And I need help up. Please don't look," she repeated, feeling ridiculous.

Ed pulled her up off the toilet, helping her regain her balance. He walked her slowly back to the hide-away bed in the living room. He stoked the fire in the fireplace again, and placed Dawn's old cast iron teapot that she'd picked up at a tag sale decades ago on the fire.

"I'm going to make you some tea to settle your stomach," he explained. "The snow seems to have slowed. I've got to try and get the walkway shoveled so we can get you to the hospital. Do you think you'll be okay for an hour or so?" Dawn nodded, feeling the love she'd felt for her husband in her drunken stupor last night fill her up again, and she smiled at him. He returned her emotional beam with a slow grin. "Maybe later, if you're up to it, we can get frisky again," he chuckled, and her smile froze. Here she was feeling lucky to have someone so thoughtful take care of her in her time of need, and Ed was thinking about getting laid.

"Go shovel," she grumbled, and pulled the sheets up to her chin.

Dawn napped fitfully, her body instinctively trying to

curl up in a fetal position, the wooden planks fighting her impulses and sending hot, angry bolts of pain to her knee each time she moved. She woke to a cold living room and no Ed. Her head felt better, and she propped herself up on her elbows, calling out for her husband.

"Ed? Are you in the basement? I need help getting up." She was not enjoying having to be dependent on her husband just to get in and out of bed, and she hoped the hospital would tell her nothing was broken or torn when she got there and the splints were an overreaction. She pushed back the covers and examined her leg. Her knee and calf were fatly swollen; she could see bruising around her ankle joint and along the arch of her foot. Her kneecap seemed to be resting a little to the right of where it should be; it was hard to tell among the puffiness, but she was pretty sure it was off-kilter. "Ed?" she called again, and struggled to push herself up. She settled onto the crutches and made her way slowly to the picture window that looked out over the front walkway.

Dawn pushed the curtains aside. Ed had managed to shovel halfway down the walk. He was facedown in the snow bank next to the walkway, the handle of his red shovel angling up out of the snow next to him. "Ed!" Dawn lurched toward the front door. She threw it open and maneuvered onto the stoop, wearing nothing but her thin pajamas and fuzzy purple bedroom slippers. She hobbled out to him as fast as she could, crutches sliding in the slickness of the shoveled pathway. She tried to lean over him and lost her balance, falling on top of him. She quickly rolled over into the snow bank beside him, and pushed his shoulder back. Ed's face was blue; his eyes were wide open, snow sticking to the glassy orbs. Dawn used her fingers to scoop the thin film of flakes from his eyes. He remained unblinking; Dawn put her head down against his chest, listening for his strong, steady heartbeat. There was only silence.

Dawn screamed, shaking her husband's shoulder. His head lolled back and forth in response, but he did not start breathing. Dawn folded her body as best she could around his head to warm him up, rocking him.

She became aware some time later of the coldness permeating her backside. Someone was keening, a horrible, heartbreaking howl, and she realized the sound was coming from herself. She tried to cough the iciness out of her chest, and peered down at her husband again. His face was still blue; his eyes still unseeing. She sobbed, and placed his head gently back on the snow. He was too heavy for her to move. She had to call 911, hoping against hope he was merely suffering hypothermia and the paramedics could bring him back. She swung herself back into the house on the crutches and searched frantically for the cell phone. She finally spotted it on the basement stairs, where Ed had left it the night before. Dawn leaned forward, and felt her center of balance shift. She couldn't get down there on the crutches. She sat with a hard thump, scooting down the stairs on her fanny. She reached the phone and dialed; Linda's voice was suddenly next to her, asking her briskly what her emergency was. Dawn was overcome with relief to hear another person's voice, and started to cry as she explained how she'd found Ed.

"How long has he been out there?" Linda asked, and Dawn glanced at her watch for the first time since she'd woken up. Her heart sank.

"Probably four hours. My God, is that bad? I was napping—I didn't know he was out there that long," Dawn wailed.

"Stay calm, Mrs. Bloom; don't panic. I'm sending an ambulance now, but I'll be honest, I don't know if they can get to you with that long driveway and the snow. Is there any way you can get him to the street? Is there anyone you can call to dig you out?" Dawn searched her mind for anyone she might know with a plow.

Bob Deveraux, of course. Bob had a yellow plow on the front of his white Ford F-350.

"I'll call Bob. I have to hang up now," she told Linda, and disconnected the call. Dawn reverse-scooted back up the stairs, clutching the cell phone. She propped herself on the crutches and made her way to the end table where she kept the phone book. She found Bob's number, and dialed, her hands shaking; it took a full minute of the phone ringing endlessly for her to realize that if her power was out, most likely, Bob's was too. She didn't have a cell phone number for him.

Dawn swallowed hard. She'd have to make her way over to Bob's house, a half mile away. On crutches. In two feet of snow.

She found Jimmy's old quilted coveralls in the hall closet. He'd worn them on skiing trips, and had tucked thermal gloves and a bright orange knit cap in the pockets. Dawn bundled herself up carefully. The coveralls were tight over the wood planks and her hips, but she could still zip it all the way up, which was all that mattered. She had to take care of Ed now. He needed her.

She looked around for supplies, and filled a backpack with bottled water for her trek. She slipped her cell phone into the breast pocket; the battery was at twenty-nine percent, so she made a mental note to use it sparingly. She knew she'd be slow with her twisted knee and the crutches, but she didn't think she'd need much in the way of food. It was only a half a mile, for goodness sake. If the weather were perfect and she had full use of her legs, it would only take her ten minutes to walk to Bob's; she was guessing she would be at his front door in a half an hour at most.

Dawn swung past Ed down the pathway, steadying herself on the crutches. "I'll be back with help, honey. You hang in there." She didn't want to see her husband, his stillness, but she glanced back at him quickly. He remained where she'd left him, staring up at the sky. She turned away, hot tears starting again, and took her first step into the snow.

Dawn soon came to realize she had grossly underestimated how long it would take her to get to the Deveraux house. She was wading through the heavy powder, her crutches abandoned; the high drifts were helping to support her, and the cold set in quickly, causing her knee to go numb. Occasionally she would twist the wrong way, and a jolt of pain would make her wince, but she continued to move forward, wriggling her body back and forth through the snow. She was exhausted thirty minutes out; she looked back to see how far she'd gotten and her heart sank. She could still see the house and Ed's jacket, blue against the white.

Dawn's hair was wet with sweat under her cap; she stopped a moment to pull it off and let the bitter breeze cool her. She stepped forward and cried out as her foot stopped short, hitting a large boulder hidden in the drifts; she heard the splint Ed had made for her snap. The pain was unbearable, and for a moment, she retched. Dawn panted, trying to breathe through her pain. She looked around for an area with less snow to unzip her insulated overalls and assess the damage, but she was surrounded by a wall of white. She pushed her back into the snow and tried to create a little burrow. This resulted in Dawn trying to make something of a snow angel with her three good limbs, and she laughed at herself, a hysterical sort of giggle that didn't sound like calm, sensible Dawn at all. She bit her lip to make herself stop.

Dawn leaned into her snow angel and unzipped the coveralls, trying to keep any slush from dampening her dry clothes underneath. Wrestling the fabric to the side, she got a look at the broken splint. A thin, jagged piece of wood stuck out almost perpendicular to her knee. The end of the piece was buried in her flesh. A purple ring of blood formed under the skin where the splinter punctured her skin. Dawn felt the bile rise in her throat again, and she threw up in the snow.

It had to be pulled out. She couldn't continue to wade through the snow with the wood fragment sticking out of her knee. Sighing heavily, Dawn resigned herself to yanking it out quickly, allowing herself to yell a string of curse words as she ripped the splinter out. She could hear her mother in her head, giving her a disapproving *Tsk! Language!* Dawn didn't care. It fucking hurt.

She packed her knee with snow and waited for the waves of pain to stop. It would be so easy to give up and close her eyes right here among the drifts. Dawn allowed her lids to drop for a moment, and the gummy smile of her granddaughter Jenny, who had just lost her front teeth two weeks ago, rose up in her mind. Her eyes flew open again and she struggled to stand. Her two sons needed her to go on. She had to try and do whatever she could for their father. If she didn't go on, the blizzard would claim her life, too, and she wanted to hug her granddaughter, just one more time.

Dawn plowed on, forging a slow, limping path through the wall of snow. Her house was out of sight now, her husband's prone body no longer visible. She stopped to take a sip of water and found herself drinking half the bottle in one gulp. Despite the frigid temperatures, Dawn was burning up. She tried to focus on getting to Bob: *he* would save them. Surely neighborly differences would fall to the wayside when he heard what had happened, of Ed laying in the drifts, unblinking. Just one look at her twisted frame, the blood seeping through her snowsuit, the raw desperation in her eyes . . .

As she pressed on, she thought about Ed. She knew, deep down in her heart, he was gone. If he'd just been hypothermic, he would've been able to respond to her somehow. He should've blinked when she rolled him over to face the sun. Squeezed her hand. Something.

Dawn wanted to cry again, but she was afraid to start in case the tears froze her eyes shut. She forced herself to think about the boys. Would Jimmy be trying to call to see if they came through the storm okay? Had Marty even heard about the blizzard going on up north?

Dawn found she could no longer will her leg with the

bad knee to move forward and started to crawl, keeping her mangled leg as straight as possible, using her upper arms to pull herself along. She was gulping air, her body heaving with her efforts to get more oxygen into her system, when she startled a rabbit that had been crouching in the snow. It bounded off, letting her eyes follow the creature as it made its escape, and spotted color up ahead. Bob's blue-shingled house. Her heart soared as she crawled faster, wriggling her way toward salvation. He'd plowed the drive in front of his house and shoveled a path to his front door. Dawn burst out of the snowdrift to the cleared drive and started hopping on one leg, each jump causing a spike of heated pain to radiate through her aching knee. The stretch of path to Bob's door seemed to take forever, and she sat down again, scooting on her rear end up the walkway like a child, unable to hold up her weight for one more moment. Leaning on the corner of his storm door, she used her teeth to pull off her thermal gloves, and started banging.

"Bob! Bob! Please help; *please*. I need you."

Dawn sat on the front step for a few minutes, alternating between thumping on the door and shouting. She could hear no movement inside. If she had to, she would break into the house and try and find the keys to his truck. She would drive with her one good leg if necessary. She had to get the ambulance to her husband. She hefted herself up, using the door handle for support, and tried the knob. It was unlocked, and she hopped inside.

"Crazy hooligans. I've a right to protect my property," Bob slurred, and Dawn looked up to see her cantankerous neighbor weaving slightly on his feet, pointing a shotgun directly at her. The smell of alcohol hit her a second later. She threw her hands in the air.

"Bob, it's me, it's Dawn Bloom. I'm not here to rob you, I need he—" The shotgun blast cut off her plea. The wood frame of the doorway next to her splintered, and she ducked quickly, sliding back out the door in one swift motion. The crazy bastard was trying to kill her!

Dawn propped herself against the side of Bob's house, looking around for something to help support her weight. She was cold, and wet, and her whole body and soul ached. This rotten prick was not going to shoot her now, when she was so close to escaping the white drifts that had caused all of her problems to begin with. She spotted a snow shovel leaning a few feet away from her, and reached for it, ready to use it as a crutch.

The front door was still wide open, and she heard Bob grumbling inside.

And moving. Toward her.

Gripping the shovel, she pressed her body flat against the shingles.

"Come back here, you damn hooligan! I'll sho' you who's boss around here!" Dawn heard him approach. Looking down at her own mangled knee, she realized she knew exactly how to take care of Bob.

He appeared in the doorway, and Dawn swung. The corner of the metal snow shovel caught Bob right in the kneecap, and he doubled over, howling. She hit him again, this time in the head, and he dropped his shotgun and went down, cursing a blue streak, clutching his knee, and rolling on the front step.

"Where are your keys, Bob?" Dawn asked coldly. She

could no longer feel her own knee. Her sympathy had also gone numb.

"Why'd ya do a thing like that? Crazy bitch!"

"Your keys, Bob. Or I take out your other knee."

"Screw you," Bob slurred through clenched teeth, and Dawn raised up the shovel again, bringing it straight down on Bob's right leg, aiming for the joint. She'd never heard a grown man shriek before. She kind of liked it.

"Looks like you need to get to a hospital, Bob. Where are your keys?"

He blinked up at her for a moment. Bob fished keys out of his pocket, handing them over with a shaky hand.

"Please," he whined, seeming to forget who had caused his injuries to begin with. "I think I can get to the passenger side if you let me lean on you."

Dawn tried to smile, but the sides of her mouth disagreed and pulled down. "I feel your pain, I really do. But you just tried to kill me. My husband's dead, I can't feel my legs, and I'm starting to suspect the blood I'm losing from the puncture wound in my own broken knee is going to cause me problems. Screw *you*, Bob," she finished, tucking the snow shovel under her arm.

Dawn hobbled to Bob's truck gingerly, feeling dizzy. She let out a yelp as she slid behind the wheel, a hot shock of pain reminding her that she was not completely whole, maybe never would be again. The truck was reluctant to turn over. She tried again, and when the engine caught and held, she cried.

Her first stop would be the hospital, that much she knew. But once she made it through this, once her husband was buried and she was off crutches and healed, she had one more stop to make, before she moved to warmer climes, maybe Florida.

Dawn thought she just might take her new snow shovel and pay a visit to one Roland van Berg on her way out of town.

MAX ELLIOTT, EXTERMINATOR

Max Elliott was an exterminator. He'd cleared zombies out of entire towns in his prime, severing spinal cords and sending undead heads rolling without breaking a sweat. His weapon of choice was his machete, which he was using now to clean out the dirt under his fingernails, reclining with his boots up on the dusty table in his little cottage.

Once the vaccine had eliminated the zombie plague, Max had found himself out of a job. Devastated cities were being rebuilt, zombie hordes were rounded up and cured or disposed of, and trees were being planted along neighborhood streets. Max was a fighter, not a builder, and he'd found himself with little to do, a zombie slayer with no one to decapitate. He sat now, waiting for a knock at the door, calling him to action once again.

The knock came.

Max opened the door to his red-faced neighbor, a portly woman who owned the cottage down the road. She was panting, having rushed at a high waddle to reach Max's bungalow.

"Come quick," gasped the woman, pulling her fists up to her mouth with a yelp. "It's a nightmare! They've taken over the whole garden!"

Max turned and spat, his saliva tinged brown from the wad of tobacco resting between his cheek and jaw. He patted his pocket to reassure himself he had enough Copenhagen to carry him through this new mission, then turned back to the neighbor and smiled. Brown flecks of chaw stuck in his teeth.

"What seems to be the problem, ma'am?" he drawled.

The neighbor shuddered. "Aphids," she squeaked.

Max Elliott, exterminator, was back in the saddle again.

PEOPLE PERSON

Jess moved to the island on a lark, answering an ad that promised "Summer jobs—fun in the sun!" She was working at the island grocery store, and from Memorial Day to Labor Day, the lines stretched to the back of the shop, where the deli hawked sandwiches and pickles. Her register was the old-fashioned type, into which she still had to manually punch the prices and departments, and half of the time, the keys stuck. The customers were hot and sticky and eager to take their overpriced chips and sodas to the beach, and Jess enjoyed every minute of it. She loved meeting new people. She thought of it as an adventure, and every face she saw held a story to be read, a fresh perspective on the tiny ocean town.

Jess had straight brown hair she kept pulled back in a ponytail, and sea green eyes. Her love of fine foods kept her constantly battling her weight, but this summer, she was winning the fight against being a fatty. She found many of the tourists that filtered through her line would flirt and banter with her, but the locals seemed more reserved. Their conversations with her were stilted and cautious; Jess would just smile at them, assuming that time would win them over. She had a small apartment above the store, and when the manager asked if she would consider staying the winter and keeping the room, she thought she might. She was estranged from her parents, having disappointed them by graduating college as a culinary arts major instead of following in Daddy's footsteps and becoming a lawyer. When she'd announced her major her sophomore year, her parents had yelled, screamed, cried, and eventually pulled all financial support. She had college loans to pay off, and the island might provide the kind of solitude and inspiration she needed to concentrate on her cooking. She agreed to stay on.

After Labor Day, the island shut down like a hermit crab withdrawing into its shell. Storefronts were boarded up; restaurants went dark; the theater sat vacant. Jess found herself with time to spare at the register, often reading a magazine or flipping through a cookbook between customers. The faces that came in became familiar to her, and she learned from these locals that only about 200 people stayed year-round. It was isolated and cold on the island in winter, but Jess thought she might welcome that. She took to wandering the beach after work, combing the tidewater line for hidden treasures left by the sea. She had a tidy little kitchen in her apartment, and took to experimenting with spices and herbs, indulging her creative cookery. She had a television and a laptop in her room, but her Internet connection was spotty at best, so she didn't keep in touch with her friends from school as often as she would've liked. She e-mailed her brother, Stephen, occasionally, to let him know how she was, but after he unfriended her on Facebook, she didn't bother trying with him anymore. She understood. Stephen was in his second year of law school at Boston University, working hard to be just like Daddy, and couldn't risk their parents' wrath by staying in contact with her.

As fall descended, the boat schedule slowed to a standstill, offering one boat a day, then every other day, until the islanders had only the Saturday morning ferry as an option to get to the mainland. The only places open were the grocery, the post office, the gas station, one church, and one local pub. She'd ventured in to the bar a couple of times, just for human contact. Each person in the place was hunched over a beer, so she'd ordered a Budweiser to fit in. The man next to her (who smoked Pall Malls, she remembered from the store) smiled at her, introducing himself as Phil. He was in construction, had lived on the island twelve years, and what was a nice girl like her doing in a place like this? Jess had stammered, her tongue not yet loosened by the ale, and Phil had taken this as an invitation to continue.

"Not much for a young gal like yourself to do out here, is all." He shrugged, sipping his beer. Foam stuck to the coarse gray beard growing wild on his face.

"I guess that's why I came in here for a drink." Jess frowned. "What *is* there to do out here all winter?"

"Come to the bar!" Phil said with a laugh, drawing it out, waiting for her to join in. She gave a nervous chuckle, and he continued. "Seriously, folks here either come to the bar, or go to church and talk about the people at the bar.

Some don't bother to leave their house at all," he added.

"Sounds lonely," Jess mused, sipping her beer. "Don't they miss being around people? Does anyone go visit them?" Phil gave her a long look from under his dark, bushy brows, and started to slowly rub his thumb, which was missing its top knuckle.

"Some people just don't like other folks is all. Best you leave those types be. Don't go disturbin' people who don't want disturbin'."

Jess flashed her widest smile and stood.

"Me, I'm a people person," she'd grinned, feeling a little giggly after the beer. "I wouldn't be able to stand being shut in all winter. I'll see you at the store, Phil."

Sometimes, when she was walking down the beach, she would catch a glimpse of something moving in the dunes, a flash of color out the corner of her eye. As the days grew shorter and the beaches fell to darkness earlier, she thought she saw shining sets of eyes glowing at her from the dunes. There were no coyotes or raccoons on the island; she began to imagine spooks and werewolves were watching, waiting to make her one of their own. The idea strangely thrilled her, but no creatures jumped out to bite.

Jess began sleeping with Cobb out of loneliness. He was too old for her, probably twenty years her senior, though she hadn't bothered to ask him his age. He had short, graying blond hair and tanned forearms. When he crinkled his eyes in a smile he oozed charm; she imagined she was not the first girl fresh out of college to tumble into bed with him.

"Why aren't you with someone?" she asked, watching him putter around the kitchen, naked, in search of coffee.

"My last girl left the island. Couldn't take it out here." He found the coffee, poured two steaming mugs, and offered her one. Jess accepted it gratefully, then began tracing a circle on his pale, muscled leg after he sat.

"Does that happen a lot? People up and leaving without warning?"

"Happens all the time. You young kids, you come out here, think you're going to be the next Picasso or Hemingway, then once the ferries stop running, you can't handle being cut off from Mommy and Daddy. You probably won't make it past December," he added with a wave of his mug. Jess was mildly offended, but didn't correct him.

"Why do you stay?" The circle on his leg grew wider, the loop more pronounced.

"I'm a good hunter." He grinned, and thumped the graying curls on his chest twice for emphasis. "Tarzan hunt and fish. Provide for his woman." She giggled, and they wound up folding themselves back under the blanket, and her loneliness was eased, for a while.

Cobb showed her how to surf cast and taught her how to fillet a fish. She'd tried this on her own in the past, but would invariably end up with a bony mess. He pointed out mushrooms and berries to avoid as they hiked the island's nature trails; she was eager to learn how to live off the land. When deer season opened up, she crouched with him in his deer stand, waiting motionlessly until her legs went numb for a young buck or fattened doe to wander down the path. She was a crack shot, and Cobb praised her; he patiently demonstrated how to hang the doe she'd bagged, letting the blood drip down toward the snout so as not to spoil the meat. She spent hours in the kitchen, perfecting her venison stew; Cobb invited some of the locals to her tiny apartment to taste her wares. She tried to fit in, be a part of the small, tight-knit (if slightly odd) community; but there was always a look, or a comment by an islander, to let her know that although she'd stuck it out so far, she still didn't belong.

There was a chill in the air the morning Jess showed up to the grocery ten minutes late, her cheeks still flushed from the moments she'd been outside in the single-digit winds, running down the back stairs from her apartment to the rear door of the store. She rubbed her hands together and walked back to the deli, where the store manager was prepping the meats for the day.

"Sorry I'm late, boss," she offered, heading to the coffee pot to pour a cup. "The power must've gone out last night, 'cause my alarm never went off."

"I need to talk to you, Jess," her manager said, a steely edge to his words. "I have to lay you off for the winter. I thought there would be a place for you here, but the store can't support this many employees."

"This many?" Tears welled up in Jess's eyes. "There're three of us! What am I supposed to do?"

Her manager shook his head. "I can give you 'til Saturday in the apartment. That way you'll have time to pack before the ferry comes."

"But—what about today? Don't you want me to work my shift?" Jess was hurt and confused.

"Your shift's covered. You can go back upstairs and start packing. I'm sorry," he added, a half-hearted afterthought.

Jess wandered to the front of the store, where she saw

a young blonde behind the register. One of the locals' daughters, she realized. She'd been fired so the island could support their own.

Jess left the store, hot tears blurring her eyes, and went in search of Cobb. He'd stayed on his boat last night, as he often did when she had to work early, and she went down to the west dock to see if he was up and fishing yet. She needed a shoulder to cry on, plus, he might be able to help her stay on the island for the winter. Maybe she could live on the boat with him.

The old wooden trawler was painted a deep hunter green, and was tied up to a faded gray pier with warped boards. She approached slowly, a growing dread forming in the pit of her stomach. She could hear faint groaning coming from below deck, and for a moment, the eyes in the dunes flickered in her mind.

She stepped onboard cautiously, not wanting to make a sound to alert the creature below of her presence. The groaning grew louder, and Jess shuddered—no mortal creature was capable of these guttural noises.

She untied a short gaff from the deck and slunk to the door that led below, slowly creeping down the stairs. She lifted her weapon back, ready to strike the ungodly beast that sounded like it was rending her boyfriend to bits. It took a moment for her eyes to focus on the shapes in the room; she recognized Cobb, naked, pumping steadily, a head of frizzy gray hair entwined in his fingers. Jess thought she recognized the woman, the bartender at the local bar. It was from this woman the groaning sounds came; she was howling and moaning intermittently as Cobb kept his rhythm going. Jess slapped her hand to her mouth quickly, afraid to make a noise, and backed up the stairs slowly, then turned and fled.

Jess ran down the beach, her quiet place, hot tears streaming down her face. She would never fit in here. Her employer had rejected her; now her boyfriend was sleeping around on her with a local. Everyone she turned to—her parents, her brother, her lover—was telling her she wasn't wanted in their world. Would she *ever* find a place to fit in? Her despair quickly turned to anger. She'd tried. She was a goddamn *people* person, chatting with everyone; hell, she'd even invited them into her home and fed them. The problem wasn't her: it was *them*.

If they didn't want her, she mused, slowing her pace to a jog, well, she could give them a reason, at least.

She wasn't a bad person. But she could be.

She was leaving on Saturday's ferry, so she invited half the island to her apartment Friday afternoon. Jess no longer cared enough to be humiliated by the fact that she was throwing her own going-away party. She cooked all day, getting permission from her former manager to use the grocery's deli stove and cooking pots to make vats of her specialty stew. She had plenty of beer on hand, a sure guarantee people would show up. A large crowd of mostly strangers filtered in and out of her apartment; she was embarrassed at how few faces she knew after living on the island for six months already.

"Where'd Cobb get off to?" Phil asked. She smiled thinly. Cobb, or what remained of him, was scattered to the sea. She'd asked to go hunting with him yesterday afternoon, never letting on that she knew about his nooner with the bartender. She'd waited until they were deep in the brush, then slit his throat with his own filleting knife. She'd used one of his own deer hangers to drain the blood from his body before skinning and processing the meat. Her muscles still throbbed from the effort, but all in all, the stew had come out smelling delicious.

"Haven't seen him in a few days. Maybe he decided he couldn't take it out here anymore." Jess shrugged, then offered Phil a bowl. "Eat up!"

Jess stopped by the local paper on her way to the ferry dock the next morning. It was a foggy sunrise, and the newspaper office hadn't opened yet, wouldn't unlock their doors for another couple of hours. She left a copy of her stew recipe tucked in to the box outside the office door. She figured the mushrooms she'd added to the stew had kicked in sometime during the night; she'd been careful to select only the mushrooms with white gills—*death caps*, Cobb had called them on their nature hikes. She whistled as she pulled her pink wheeled suitcase to the ferry dock. She figured she could move on to someplace new, maybe find a place where the locals weren't so cold and mean.

She was a people person, after all.

MOTHER'S DAY

Ella woke with a sigh, rolling over and pulling the black comforter up to her chin. Eyes closed, she felt around the other side of the bed; hearing no corresponding "oof!" to her pawing, she knew John was already up and puttering around the house. Ella blinked, remembering—today was Mother's Day, and she had to go visit Mama.

Ella shuffled into the bathroom and began her morning ritual: wash her face, brush her teeth, shower, apply makeup, dry and style her hair. She started humming as she flossed, a flawed rendition of "It's My Party," but who was around to hear? At sixty, Ella was pretty proud of her trim, petite figure, and having been raised by a true Southern belle, had been trained to always look her best. She pulled on a neatly ironed white Ann Taylor blouse and powder blue capris, letting her fingers slide down her belly, sighing at her meno-pot. She'd never lose that paunch, but she blamed genetics more than fading hormones. Ella came from a long line of round-bellied women, and had learned to accept rather than fight it.

She ran a rounded brush through her short bob, squinting at the silver that she'd allowed to snake through her light brown hair. Mama wouldn't like it, she knew, but to hell with Mama. She was dead, and Ella was still learning how to relax now that she was free from her mother's criticism.

Ella and her mother had been close, but Ella never felt like she'd lived up to her mother's standards. Mama would complain that Ella was too short, insisting she wear heels at all times as a teenager—but not those "trashy platform things" her friends were wearing. Her hair should be long, because that's what the boys liked, and any extra allowance or pin money should immediately be invested in Mary Kay products. Mama had frowned at Ella's ambitions to be a teacher, and was thrilled when Ella quit her job tutoring kids in English as a second language upon becoming pregnant. Mama had discouraged Ella from returning to work after Amy was born; having a career wasn't important in Mama's eyes. Hydrating to keep one's skin supple was.

Mama had so many rules and tips on how a proper Southern woman should live her life that Ella had found it easier to give in and live by them than to try and defy Mama. Ella's layered bob hairdo was the first time in her life she could remember trying to wriggle out from under her mother's thumb, and even then, she'd waited until Mama had been dead for three months before she'd dared to try it.

Ella formed an O with her mouth and applied a coat of lavender lipstick. Mama had been dead now for seven months, but Ella still felt the trickling tentacles of guilt her mother had wielded like a weapon. Daddy had died when Ella was ten, due to complications of "the diabetes," as Mama liked to say. She barely remembered him, only that he was always laughing, a man who enjoyed a good joke. Nobody would've appreciated it more that Ella had married a man with the last name Fitzgerald.

Ella critiqued her appearance in the mirror and was satisfied that her makeup and hair were perfectly set. She grabbed her traveling cosmetic case to tuck into her purse—she never left home without it—and made her way to the kitchen to look for John.

Ella found coffee brewing, but no husband. She moved to the window above the sink and peered outside. There was a thin cloud of smoke coming from behind the garage. John was sneaking cigars again; why that man thought she couldn't smell it every time she got into the car or sorted his clothes for the laundry was beyond her. She thought for a moment about how she would react today. Indignant? Hurt? Angry he was cutting his life short, leaving her without someone to mow the lawn or hold her hand at the movies? She decided to ignore it, yet again. She wasn't up to the task of lecturing John on the harmful side effects of tobacco use; she had to mentally prepare herself for the cemetery.

Mama had started complaining about headaches last June. Ella faithfully visited her mother every weekend; she and John had moved just five miles down the road from Mama's pecan plantation in Willingham, South Carolina. Ella had become alarmed when just a few weekends later she noticed her mother slurring; Mama didn't drink as a rule, and there wasn't a drop of liquor in the house. When Mama admitted she was having trouble writing—keeping up correspondence with the extended family was a priority for her, and something she did faithfully, though she considered e-mail crass and an unacceptable form of communication—Ella had insisted she go to a doctor. Mama was diagnosed with an inoperable brain tumor the first week of July. They tried everything, from chemotherapy to homeopathy and macrobiotics, but Mama, once a strong, sturdy woman, grew weaker before her eyes. In a last-ditch effort to get well, Mama had even enrolled in a trial biochemical therapy program, though her doctor strongly advised against it, referring to the scientists behind the experimental treatment as "radical, blood-sucking quacks" and "steaming piles of chemo-induced vomit." For a while, despite Dr. Cooper's gloomy warnings, Mama rallied, seeming to get physically stronger even as her body wasted away, but in the end, it was all for naught. Mama died on Halloween, managing to open her watery eyes on her deathbed, pat Ella's hand with her own skeletal one, and tell her she really ought to do something with her hair. Ella loved her mama, but Lord, that woman was never happy!

She heard John approaching and poured herself and him a cup of coffee. He let the entryway door close with a bang as he came in, quickly shedding his flannel shirt in the doorway, perhaps hoping the cigar smell would cling to it and not him. He was wearing an old UCONN tee shirt—John grew up in Connecticut, and though he hadn't lived there since high school, hadn't even attended college at the University of Connecticut, he still had a fierce loyalty to their women's basketball team. She smiled as he leaned over and gave her a quick peck on the cheek, smoothly reaching for his mug of coffee as he did it. John had worked as a finish carpenter all his life, and since retiring, he'd put on twenty pounds, and let his blond hair grow long. His beard still felt funny against her cheek. She handed him the hazelnut-flavored creamer and moved to the kitchen table.

John Fitzgerald was a good-looking man; he'd been cute in college, where they'd met when they found themselves sitting next to each other in French class. Over the years, as he grew wider, more muscled, and more weathered, John had grown handsome, and he often reminded her of Jeff Bridges, especially now, with the shaggy hair and beard.

John was her touchstone, and she was constantly amazed at how lucky she'd been that he'd fallen in love with her. For every criticism Mama had over her choice of nail polish shade or how she loaded the dishwasher incorrectly, John was right beside her, reminding her how unimportant these barbs really were.

"You have your own family now," he would say. "And we think you're perfect. Who cares if that platter wasn't dishwasher safe? It came out in one piece; that's all that matters." When she tried to point out the slight warp and the water stains, he'd silence her with a kiss.

"Amy call yet?" John asked as he slid into the chair across from her. Amy was their daughter, now thirty-six and living in upstate New York, working as an attorney. She was happily married to a fellow attorney, with no children, something Mama had bitterly complained about in the last years of her life.

"What's wrong with her? Why am not a great-grandmamma yet? Who raised that girl to think a career was more important than giving me a great-grandchild?"

Mama knew darn well who'd raised Amy, and Ella'd shaken her head, not even bothering to defend herself yet again. "Give her time, Mama. There's still time."

But there hadn't been time, and now Mama was gone, and Ella, free from her mother's barbs that had been such a part of her everyday life, was beginning to think maybe she wasn't such a failure in life. Her husband ("It's because you insisted on going to college that you wound up having to marry a Yankee," her mother had groused. "Good Southern men don't want their wives to be worrying about education"). Her daughter ("I don't know how she's going to be a lawyer when she doesn't even have the sense God gave geese, moving up north like that," Mama had lamented). Even herself ("Now you know, Ella, you aren't as pretty as those other girls, and you sure aren't as smart, either. Miss Betty's etiquette classes and my makeup tips are about the only thing you're going to have going for you if you want to make it in this world"). Without her mother around to point out all of the mistakes she'd made, Ella could see things as they really were: she'd married a kind, hardworking, and loving man; together they'd raised a brilliant, beautiful daughter, and Ella had done all right with the life she'd made for herself. The fact that she and John were now mostly living off of the proceeds of the sale of Mama's pecan farm made her happy life despite Mama's disapproval all the sweeter.

Ella felt a wave of guilt wash over her. Mama had done

the best she could, Ella knew. Mama hadn't wanted children, so when she got pregnant at forty, right when she'd been looking forward to easing into her menopause years, it was a shock. Ella knew her mother had loved her. She just didn't *like* Ella that much.

"Going to the cemetery today?" John's question interrupted her thoughts, and she nodded, feeling ashamed. She hadn't been to the cemetery in a month, a far cry from the promise she'd made Mama to continue to visit her every week. The last time she'd been there, she'd had to call the groundskeeper and complain. The ground above Mama's grave had been spongy and soft, like something had been digging it up from below. Surely the groundskeeper had something in his bag of tricks to control the mole activity in the graveyard? It was disrespectful to the dead, Ella felt, and she hoped that the rodent problem had been resolved at Green Lawn.

"I'm going in a little bit," Ella said, sipping her coffee. "Got some things to do around the house. Plus, I want to wait for Amy to call." John stood, eyes sparkling.

"Almost forgot. Got something for you." He went back to the entryway off the kitchen, and crouched behind the door. He came back carrying a large pot with what appeared to be a stick poking out of it. "Happy Mother's Day." He grinned. "It's a cherry tree."

Ella oohed and aahed over the gift, remarking how sweet he was to remember she loved cherries. The tree was tiny; it would never grow big enough to produce fruit in her lifetime, but Ella fussed over it just the same. He had a good heart, her husband did. She gave him a long kiss, then held him for a minute, listening to his heart thump solidly in his chest. She had a good life, she knew. Despite what her mother'd thought.

Ella made her way through the chores, sorting a week's worth of laundry, sweeping the floors, dusting the corners of each room. She was watching a rerun of *Matlock* and ironing when she finally checked the time and gasped. It was nearly five, and she'd forgotten all about Mama.

"Gotta run!" she shouted to John, who was out back, admiring the fine job he'd done planting the cherry tree. "Cemetery closes at dusk!" Ella drove quickly to the graveyard, stopping to run into Ingle's Market and grab a bouquet of flowers. She breathed a sigh of relief as she pulled through the cemetery gates, slowly making her way down toward the newer section, where Mama lay.

Parking on the side of the paved path, she undid her seatbelt and pulled down her visor. Ella quickly applied a fresh coat of Lasting Lavender, then fished out her brush to tidy her hair. She sprayed a fine mist of her travel-size Aqua Net hairspray, and then used her hands to smooth the last flyaway hairs into place. She felt a little bit silly getting dolled up just to visit her mother's grave, but she figured that wherever Mama was, she would appreciate it.

Ella climbed out of the car, clutching her bouquet. Mama was buried in the middle of the row, just a few feet from a large pink mimosa tree. Ella spied a hummingbird darting among its fronds, and smiled. She'd forgotten how pretty it was here, and was glad she'd come.

Ella found her mother's grave quickly, and knelt to brush away some brown grass clippings covering the stone.

"Hi, Mama, sorry I'm late," she whispered, placing the spring flowers next to the marker. "I know you'd prefer daisies, but it was the best I could do." She traced her mother's name, Charlotte Shelby Suffield, with her fingers as she talked. "Everyone's fine. Amy's still in New York, and John's doing well," she went on. "John's thinking about building a shed out back for his gardening tools and such. Mama, you wouldn't believe how he's been planning and planting since he retired. Who knew he'd turn in to a regular Martha Stewart once he had time on his hands?" Ella's laugh cut off sharply with a scream. A grisly, bony hand had shot up from the spongy earth and clamped onto her wrist, the fingertip bones digging in to her skin. "Mama! Mama, help!"

The ground seemed to erupt then, dirt flying everywhere. Ella had a brief flashback to a horror movie John had taken her to when Amy was ten and they'd wanted to have a date night. In the movie, a bunch of children had murdered all of the parents in their town, as a sacrifice to the devil. The earth below her now funneled up as it had in that movie, when Satan had come to take the leader of the children away to hell. "It's Satan, Mama! Satan!" Ella shrieked, backing away from her mother's gravesite as best she could with the dirty hand still attached to her wrist. Ella looked down and saw it was attached to whatever was coming out of the grave. She wrenched her arm free, and heard a finger, then two, snap at the force. "Jesus protect me!" she hollered, running to the car, hitting the unlock button on her remote as she fled, clutching her pocketbook.

Ella yanked the door open and threw herself inside, banging it shut and locking it as fast as she could. Tears and dirt streaked her face, and she put her head down on the steering wheel for a moment, trying to calm her breathing. Satan or no, she couldn't drive anywhere if she was hyperventilating.

Ella felt around for her keys. She'd *just* had them in her hand. Where had she put them? She patted herself down frantically. She wouldn't have thrown them in her purse. She must have dropped them. Ella groaned.

Peering out the window, she saw mounds of dirt around her mother's grave, but no signs of any demons or devils that might've emerged from the earth. She quietly pulled the handle of her car door, ever-so-slowly cracking it open. There! Her keys were on the ground, right by the car door; they must have slipped out of her hand when she was frantically trying to get to safety. She cautiously stuck her hand out of the bottom of the car door, reaching; just a little farther . . .

The door slammed hard on her hand, causing Ella to cry out. She looked up into the eyes of her decaying mama, groaning, slobbering, and scratching at the car window as the woman tried to get to her. Ella screeched and pulled her aching hand back in, slamming the door shut once again. Mama! Satan was *Mama*, back from the dead!

Mama moaned, finger bones scraping against glass. Something had been chewing at her eyelids, giving her hazel eyes a wide-open expression like a gruesome china doll. Her face had started to decompose, and she could see Mama's jaw through a hole in her cheek. Ella thought she caught a glimpse of the gold fillings Mama had always insisted on, shining through the rotting hole. Mama had been buried in a wig, since the chemo had robbed her of her hair, and it sat off-kilter now on Mama's rotting scalp, making Ella think of a Davy Crockett coon-skin hat. It wasn't Mama outside, she had to remind herself. The decaying, drooling zombie with its face pressed against the window, eyeing her like she was Thanksgiving dinner, wasn't her beloved mother. Mama would never behave in such an unladylike fashion.

Ella double-checked the locks on the door, then buried her face in her hands and sobbed. Why was this happening to her? She never should've had those disrespectful thoughts about the dead. She should've visited Mama's grave more often; should've reminded herself how hard Mama had worked to buy her pretty clothes and take her for manicures. Ella glanced up at the window again, where Zombie-Mama was scratching . . . scratching. Black ooze dribbled from where Ella had snapped its fingers graveside in her effort to get out of its viselike grip. *Guess Mama didn't bother to keep up with her mani-pedis since becoming one of the undead*, Ella mused, giggling nervously in spite of herself. This whole situation was ridiculous. Here she was, trapped in the Ford Focus John had bought for her last year ("you need a sensible sedan," he'd said, folding his arms over his chest in that way that meant this was a non-negotiable point. "That Crown Vic you've been driving isn't worth the repair money any more.") Her undead mother, whom she'd spent hours studying as Mama went through her full routine of Mary Kay cosmetics applied meticulously to every last eyelash, was clawing at her window, leaving ooze and spittle in her wake. Ella watched the tendons in Zombie-Mama's open cheek as they tensed and relaxed each time she snarled.

She could call John, she realized, and fished her cell

phone out of her purse. She never used the darn thing, but John insisted she carry one in case of emergencies. *Well, this is certainly an emergency*, she thought, smiling wryly, and punched in her home number. The phone beeped at her and a message appeared: NO SERVICE.

"Are you kidding, God?" she choked, and threw the cell phone on the passenger seat. "Really?"

Ella caught a glimpse of movement in her rearview mirror and gasped. The groundskeeper, an older man with a Willie Nelson-like braid in his long gray hair, was making his way over to her car, probably to tell her visiting hours were over. Dusk was upon them now, and he had actually let her stay a little later than sundown, as the last streaks of daylight were making their way across the sky. The undead creature snuffled and turned; it must've caught sight or scent of the groundskeeper as he ambled toward the Focus. Zombie-Mama squatted next to the driver's side door, waiting to pounce: Ella began to shout, pounding her hands against the glass, trying to warn the reedy figure closing in to watch out and stay away. The caretaker, apparently unable to hear Ella's frantic shouting through the glass, was coming around the trunk now; Zombie-Mama leapt up, startling the aging hippie, and Ella watched in horror as the creature bit into his neck, ripping away his throat. The blood pumped down the front of his shirt for a moment; the groundskeeper wore a stunned look as he slumped forward, dead before he hit the ground.

Ella peered through the glass outside and watched the zombie chew through the man's nose, eager to get to his brain. Her stomach clenched, and Ella strained to see if she could reach her keys while Zombie-Mama was distracted. The fiend's foot was by the door; Ella couldn't crack anything open without nudging the monster and drawing attention to herself. She noted with irony that the zombie still wore the sensible flats Ella herself had picked out for Mama's burial; they had matched best with the silver silk linen dress she'd bought special for Mama to wear in her coffin. The gown was in tatters now, hanging from the undead corpse in shreds. Ella could see the gray strap of Mama's 18-hour bra where the dress had torn away from the zombie's shoulder during its clawing ascent from the grave.

Ella was exhausted. The adrenaline rush she'd experienced for the past forty-five minutes, ever since the creature had first grabbed her at graveside, had worn her out. She closed her eyes for a minute, regretting not calling her own daughter today, even if it was Mother's Day and Amy should've picked up the phone first. She felt stupid for observing her self-imposed rules for the holiday. If she'd only called, let her know one more time how proud she was of her, how much she loved her . . .

"Eeaah! Eeeeah!"

Ella shot up in her seat. Was her mother trying to say her name? *Not her mother*. *Zombie-Mama*, she corrected. She couldn't bear to fully accept that this thing, this abomination that had resumed its task of clawing at the rubber lining of her window with blood dribbling down its chin, was her beloved mama. She didn't think she could stand it if it started calling her by name, forcing her to recognize the mama-ness that might still dwell within.

"Eeeaah!"

Ella squinted out through the pane, unable to clearly

121

see the monster on the other side. The glass was filmy, and Ella scowled; undoubtedly John was still smoking his filthy cigars in her car. She drew a line in the film with her finger, then looked at it to see a brown smudge at the tip. It wasn't that he was smoking the cigars that irritated her, it was his lying about it, saying he'd quit. If she ever got out of here—

Zombie-Mama suddenly appeared crystal-clear at the window again, pressing its half-eaten cheek against the glass. Its eyeball darted up and down, until it locked with hers. It seemed to grin then, and ran its gray tongue over its lips. Zombie-Mama gave the glass a long lick, then started its moaning again.

"Eaaaaaahhh . . ."

Ella screamed and jumped back, slamming into the center console. The hard plastic latch dug into her kidney, and she swore at the pain. What was she going to do? She needed a weapon, a way to get at her keys.

Ella looked at her palms, wondering if she could possibly fight the decaying creature leering at her through the window. She'd witnessed the zombie's strength when it had ripped open the caretaker's skull; gray matter still flecked its jowls. She didn't think she could win at hand-to-hand combat with the undead monster. She blinked, focusing on the nicotine smear still staining her finger. If John was smoking in her car, he might have a lighter hidden somewhere in here. Fire was *good*; it was the weapon of choice against Frankenstein's monster, right? Maybe it could help here. She yanked open the center console and began pulling out its contents. A Kenny Rogers CD, breath mints, loose change . . . no lighter. A search of the glove box revealed gas receipts, napkins, and a black plastic spork. Ella considered the spork a moment, then tossed it aside. She humped over the driver's seat, reaching toward the back. Ella began to pull crumpled maps out of the pocket behind the seat. Her fingers touched something rough and slightly wet, and she pulled out a half-smoked Cuban. Aha! The lighter had to be close by; a little more rummaging found her holding a green disposable BIC.

Ella began to weep with relief as she flicked it and found it working. She quickly let the flame go out, not wanting to alert Zombie-Mama to her new treasure. Twisting back around in her seat, she caught a glimpse of herself in the mirror. Her mascara had run, drawing a pattern in the crows' feet around her eyes. Her nose was red from crying, and her hairdo, so perfectly coiffed this morning, was now a ragged mess. She looked like a tired old lady. *No wonder Mama wants to kill me. I look a fright—she'd never approve.* She shook off the ridiculous thought. How was she going to fight off her mother's undead corpse? *Think!*

She glanced at her hair again, and hope sprang in her chest. Mama had told her since she was knee-high to a grasshopper she should *never* leave home without a travel-size Aqua Net. It was her brand of choice, and had been harder to find since the ozone uproar of the eighties, but it was a lesson from Mama she'd taken to heart: Ella always had hairspray with her wherever she went. She dove into her makeup bag now, fishing out the aerosol can.

"Thank you, Mama," she murmured, and looked out the window again.

Zombie-Mama was still outside, watching. It had given up trying to claw its way through the glass, and was instead slowly jiggling the door handle up and down, not giving up its efforts to make a tasty meal of Ella. Its wig had fallen off in the attack on the groundskeeper; the zombie's bald head and lidless eyes reminded Ella of a grotesque Halloween mask.

"Now or never," she muttered, moving her face close to the window. "Hey, Mama! Want a bite of this? Tasty treats, right here for ya!"

Zombie-Mama pressed her forehead against the glass and grunted.

"Eaa . . . yah," it moaned, and Ella winced. That was too close to her name for comfort.

Taking a deep breath, Ella kicked open the driver's side door, ramming the repugnant corpse in the stomach in the process. Zombie-Mama stumbled back, and Ella brought the aerosol hairspray can to eye level, placing the lighter in front of it.

"Happy Mother's Day, Mama." She lit the BIC and sprayed. A ball of fire flew at the zombie, catching the tatters of its dress. As flames licked up, the zombie began to squeal, a high-pitched shriek that reminded Ella of the time her mother had found a mouse in her kitchen. "Always one for dramatics," Ella groused, and reached down for her keys.

They were gone.

Ella's eyes flicked across the pavement in a panic. The Zombie-Mama must have kicked the keys away during its feeding frenzy. Ella squatted to the ground, scrambling. She found her keys behind the front wheel, right as her dead mother's hand dug into her shoulder. Ella spotted her mother's discarded wig on the ground and snatched it up. As she stood, she lit it on fire, turning. "Your hair's messed up, Mama. Let me fix it." Ella pulled the wig over the zombie's rotting scalp and pushed her in the chest, hard. Zombie-Mama shrieked again, wearing its grisly mask of perpetual surprise.

"Eaa-ah?"

Ella climbed back in the car quickly. The zombie reached after her, and Ella sliced off three more of its fingers as she slammed the door. The gray digits fell to the rubber mat on the floor, twitching. She stomped on them with her heel until they stopped moving.

Ella held her breath for a moment as the engine turned over. The car roared to life, and she slammed the transmission into drive and swung the Focus around, leaving tire marks in the grass. Zombie-Mama stood in front of her car, head smoking, mouth twisted in rage. Ella plowed the vehicle into her mother's burning corpse, hearing it crunch under her wheels as she bounced over it. The cemetery gates were still half open at the entrance, and Ella sped toward them, scraping her cherry-red paint job as she went flying through. She held her cell phone in one trembling hand as she drove, trying to enter in her daughter's number as she broke the speed limits in her race to get home, get away from Mama once and for all.

"Amy," she panted, getting her daughter's voicemail. "This is your mother. I want you to promise me that if I'm ever, *ever*, diagnosed with a terminal disease, you will find me a nice, clean hospice center and just let me die. I refuse," she went on, gasping for breath, "to let those radical, blood-sucking quacks put me through any crazy chemotherapy. You *promise* me, young lady, or I swear I will rise up from the dead and come after you!"

DENNY'S DILEMMA

Denny Fitzsimmons fell in love with Diane Griswold in the sixth grade. That was the year she brought in heart-shaped sugar cookies with pink icing for everyone in class to celebrate Valentine's Day. She'd slipped Denny two extra cookies, and at that moment he'd known she was his kind of girl.

Denny was built like a linebacker, with shoulders as wide as a barn. Back in sixth grade, and up through the end of sophomore year of high school, he'd been pudgy rather than solid, and he'd never worked up the courage to ask out Diane or any other girl. By the time he grew into his physique and the girls started flirting with him, Diane was already going out with Denny's best friend, Jack Bouchard. When John Cougar released "Jack and Diane" in the summer before their senior year, Denny knew there was no breaking up those two. Christ, now they had their own theme song.

Jack was a bit of a dick, Denny knew, but he had an older brother, Mickey, who would supply them with beer on the weekends, so the friendship had its merits. Jack was handsome as hell, with a charming James Dean air about him, and Denny could see why women threw themselves at him. Jack was a bad boy. And sometimes, the bad boy's best friend got his castoffs. It wasn't a bad arrangement.

Diane and Jack often hung out with Denny and whomever he was dating at the moment; the night they broke into Westwood Cemetery, it was Sarah Robbins. Sarah was tiny, with sandy blonde hair the same color as Denny's; she had a bit of a reputation, and on this very night, though Denny wouldn't know it for a few days, she would give him crabs. Mickey had procured a case of Budweiser for Jack and his friends, and the four of them cracked their beers and toasted to their senior year sitting on a blanket next to Lydia Mott's grave, b. 1860, d. 1878.

Denny slurped his brew and admired his best friend's girlfriend. Diane had crisp blue eyes and thick chestnut hair that reminded Denny of a shampoo commercial. She had a curvy figure, with smooth, tanned legs that went on forever. Her toes were painted red tonight, to match her red-striped flip-flops.

"Hey," Sarah whispered, elbowing Denny painfully in the ribs. "You look like you want to eat her for a snack."

Denny reluctantly pulled his gaze from Diane and planted a sloppy kiss on Sarah's sulking lips. They grabbed a handful of beers and wandered off behind one of the larger tombstones for a little one-on-one time.

Several Budweisers later, after Sarah had coaxed his cock to life and climbed on top of him for a sloppy round of sex, Denny found himself watching Jack and Diane through heavy lids. They seemed to be arguing, and Jack had a tight grip on Diane's wrist. She was struggling to pull free of him, and Denny thought he should get up—nobody could manhandle his Diane like that—but instead he passed out, propped up against a cold, slick tombstone.

Denny was stone cold sober in his dream, which unfolded like a serialized television episode. He saw Diane and Jack leave the cemetery, still arguing. He saw them on West Side Road, pulled over, Jack slamming his hands against the steering wheel. He was no longer upset with Diane; he was angry at himself for running out of gas. Denny watched his dream unfold with growing dread as Diane and Jack got out of the rusting red Ford Granada and leaned against the side of the car, their arms crossed, Jack's dirty brass gas can dangling in his hands. A moment later, Denny saw the headlights come around the corner, miss the turn, and slam into the side of the Granada moments after Jack leapt out of the way. Diane was folded in half between the two cars.

Denny awoke with a start, a scream still caught in his throat. He looked around for the road, for Diane's crumpled body, and it took him a moment to place himself back in the cemetery. He could hear Jack and Diane still arguing, but they'd moved out of his line of sight; Denny jumped up on unsteady feet as Sarah groaned beside him.

"Where you going, big boy?" Sarah slurred, and Denny ignored her. He had to get to Diane before she got in the car with Jack.

He caught them at the edge of the cemetery, near where the Granada was parked, half-hidden by a row of chestnut trees.

"Hey," Denny called out, afraid he wouldn't catch up in time. "You're not leaving us here?"

Jack stopped and turned to Denny. "We need to take a drive," he said icily, cigarette dangling from his lower lip. Denny caught up to the couple, breathing heavily.

"You can't," Denny said, trying to think of a way to stop them. "You'll run out of gas."

Jack snorted.

"I just filled up last week." The gas gauge in the Granada was broken, so Jack had to guess how much he'd used and how many miles he had left before filling the tank again, a trick at which he was notoriously terrible in calculating. Denny had walked a few miles with Jack's gas can on more than one occasion, and he rolled his eyes at his friend now.

"What's wrong, Denny?" Diane murmured, putting a gentle hand on his arm. "You're all pale and sweaty." Denny turned to her, desperate to keep her out of that car. His head was fuzzy and he couldn't think of a plausible lie to convince her to stay at the cemetery. He decided to go with the truth, however ridiculous it sounded.

"I had a dream. Just now. That the Granada ran out of gas on West Side and you were killed."

"What a dill weed!" Jack sneered, forcing a laugh. "You really thought that lame story would work? You just want to make goo-goo eyes with my girl. I'm tired of the way you're always mooning over her, Denny. You need to back off. Now." Jack stepped in closer to his friend, making a fist. Denny felt the anger rise in a warm rush up his spine.

"I'm trying to *help* you, jerkoff! I'm tellin' ya, I saw the two of you die. In a dream. Just now." Denny altered his vision to make it sound like Jack was in danger, too. Clearly his feelings for Diane were obvious to everyone, including his best friend, and he figured if it sounded like he was worried about Jack, too, it would play better all around. "What does it matter if it's a bogus drunken vision or not? Why even risk it?"

Jack stared at his buddy for a moment, then shook his head. He flicked his cigarette butt on the ground.

"Guess there's no harm in staying here a little longer," Jack said, and Denny exhaled, unaware he'd been holding his breath. Jack offered a tight smile. "C'mon. Let's find something to play quarters with."

The four of them wound up sleeping in the graveyard that night, waking up before the sun rose, the chilly air driving them out on the road early. The car ran out of gas halfway to Sarah's house. Diane turned around to look at Denny, shock and—was that terror?—in her eyes. Denny offered to walk for gas without grumbling. Diane was alive. That was all that mattered.

The next year flew by. High school graduation was a blur, and Jack and Denny promised to get together over the summer before Denny went off to college.

Diane had kept her distance from Denny since the night in the cemetery. She was jumpy and nervous around him, and he realized with a sinking heart that she was afraid of him. Their double dates ended, and Jack explained Diane didn't care much for Holly Head, the girl Denny had been dating since Christmas. Denny wasn't buying it for a minute, but he didn't challenge his friend. He could live with Diane being afraid of him if it meant she was okay.

Denny went on to college, drifting through majors before settling on criminal justice. He graduated and went on to the police academy in Milton, landing a job in Bradford, two towns over from where he'd grown up. Over the years he made his way up from corporal to sergeant to lieutenant. He kept fit at the gym, fighting his belly's urge to turn to flab, and it was there, on the treadmill, that he met Katrina. They dated for a year before Denny proposed, on a covered bridge in Avon, and they wed eight months later. Katrina was six months pregnant with their first child and Denny was pulling an overnight shift to help pay for the wallpaper in the nursery the evening Diane was brought in.

Denny didn't recognize her at first. It had been close to fifteen years since their high school graduation, after all. He knew he had to take the statement of a woman who'd been beaten up by her husband; they'd been called out to the house numerous times by concerned neighbors, but this was the first time the wife had agreed to press charges. When she was brought in, shuffling, head down, nothing about her triggered any bells in Denny's memory. She was heavy, and her skin was pale and gray; the index and middle fingers on her right hand were stained nicotine orange. Her yellowed bra strap showed beneath a purple tank top, and she wore faded pink sweatpants. Denny noted her brittle red hair and chestnut roots, and wondered for a moment why this woman wouldn't let her natural hair color grow out. It was a much kinder thought than his first one: *white trash*. He looked at the file in front of him. *Report of a woman screaming at 150 Peppermill Drive,*

Unit C; police responded to find wife locked in bedroom, husband in living room, heavy odor of alcohol. Bedroom door showed several dents, possibly the result of kicking. Wife refused to exit bedroom until husband was escorted out of apartment. Examination of wife reveals heavy bruising to torso and back, several defense wounds to wrists and forearms, bruising resembling fingerprints. Denny looked up at the woman sitting across from him and saw it; the mottled purple splotches all over her arms.

"Ma'am," Denny started, trying to make his voice as soothing as possible. "I'm Lieutenant Dennis Fitzsimmons. I'll be taking your statement. I know it's hard, but if you could please just go through what happened tonight, we'll do the best we can to keep you as safe as possible."

"I know you will, Denny. That's why I'm here," the woman replied, and Denny raised his eyebrows, leaning in closer to study her. The woman's sad blue eyes looked familiar, but it took him a moment. He looked down at the name again. Diane Bouchard.

"I don't believe it," he said, and he really didn't. The beautiful girl he remembered from high school couldn't possibly be the tired, defeated woman sitting across from him.

"I knew I had to see you as soon as I heard you were working here, Denny." Diane started to cry, and Denny pulled a Kleenex from the gray box on his desk and held it out awkwardly.

"My God, Diane. What happened?"

"Jack and I got married a couple years after high school. I was pregnant, so we had to. Lost the baby, though." She sniffed, blowing her nose. "Or Jack lost the baby, to put a finger on it. Got mad at me for taking the car out without permission to go to the pharmacy, punched me in the stomach 'til I passed out from the pain. Miscarried. I can't have any more," Diane added, a bubble forming in her throat, making her voice sound funny.

"My God," Denny repeated again. "I had no idea."

"Nobody did," Diane said, shaking her head. "Jack cut me off from my family, all my old friends. Made it sound like it was him and me against the world, and that he'd take care of me. Never lets me out of his sight, except when he goes to work. I can't even go to the grocery store without him, in case I buy the wrong thing," she said in a flat voice, as if yes, buying the wrong brand of sliced cheese was a mistake she was stupid enough to make. "Things got worse. We both drank more, and he hit me more. Can't hear out of my left ear," she said, pointing to the side of her head, and Denny noticed when she spoke that a tooth on the left side of her mouth, maybe three back, was missing. He stared at the bloated face of the girl who had occupied more than one fantasy in his mind, and for a moment, he was afraid he was going to cry. He breathed deep and reached forward, patting her hand.

"You're here now, Diane. It'll be okay."

"Jack told me you were a cop," Diane said, and let out a cackle. "Called you an idiot. Said if the force only knew the pranks you two pulled in high school, they never would.ve hired you."

Denny frowned. Except for the occasional game of mailbox baseball, for which they'd never been caught, Denny hadn't been that bad of a kid. Jack, however, deserved to rot in hell, and Denny's other hand, the one

Diane couldn't see behind the desk, clenched into a fist. "But I knew I had to see you," Diane continued, whispering, distraught. "Knew I'd report him the next time it happened. Knew there *would* be a next time. So here I am." She leaned in closer, so that Denny could smell the stale cigarette smoke in her brassy hair. "I had to tell you, Denny. In case you ever thought of it; ever wondered." She looked Denny square in the face, and her eyes were cold as ice.

"You should've kept your fat mouth shut that night." Her voice dropped to an angry hiss. "You should've just let me die."

WOMAN SCORNED

Linda hugged the widow without awkwardness, which she supposed was odd, considering the man in the coffin was once the love of her life, before he married Cathy. But after all, Linda *was* the one who had introduced the couple to each other.

After a perfunctory air kiss to the side of Cathy's cheek, Linda leaned in close to Seth's chalky corpse. "Sorry it didn't work out," she whispered.

***

Linda and Seth—the corpse in the coffin—first met at a pharmaceutical sales convention in Boston a little over four years ago. They were both at the bar, dodging yet another heavy-handed sales pitch, and fell into easy conversation. They fell into bed just as easily, and the next morning, over dry pastries from the hotel's continental breakfast spread, discovered they were practically neighbors back home in Connecticut. She lived in Colchester; he was just down the road in Niantic, close enough to continue the affair after the convention was over, should they so choose.

Linda so chose. The sex had been fantastic. Seth was sexy and charming, with his emerald eyes and wide Colgate smile. Linda had just turned thirty, and had made the mistake of trying a new haircut to celebrate. Her thick black curls looked terrible in an angled pixie cut, and she was still in the early stages of growing the whole mess out. Her misery had only been compounded when she'd visited Victoria's Secret and realized she'd moved up to a large in their pretty lace panty sizes. Seth was exactly what she needed to boost her spirits and feel attractive again. And that's why his smooth lies had been so easy to swallow.

During their weekend at Boston PharmaCon, there had been no mention of his wife and young son, tucked away in a townhouse off Flanders Road. He'd told her he was fresh out of the Air Force—another lie, spun to try and impress her after she'd mentioned her father had been an airman. He even shaved six years off of his age, though Linda was dumbfounded as to why he'd bothered—it certainly made no difference to her if he was thirty-two or thirty-eight. Looking back on it, she considered that she should have *known*, should've spotted the creasing crow's feet just starting to march their way across the corners of his eyes, down his cheeks—but she'd been too enamored to *want* to see it.

They continued their affair for months. She giggled and grinned every time they got together (at her place, always at her place; Seth claimed his house was such a pigsty he couldn't bear for her to see it). She gushed to her girlfriends about how wonderful he was, how he brought her flowers, and even wrote her a poem once—he was such a romantic! The nights they were apart—and there were a lot of them, what with work and obligations to parents and friends that could only be met on weekends; but on those nights, she'd examine her memories of the times they spent together, turning them over and over like a child's comfort blanket, and wonder if she was falling in love. Dared to hope that maybe he loved her, though neither had spoken of such things.

It was only when curiosity got the best of her, and she asked her friend Chandra, the wife of the Niantic tax assessor, to get her a photo of Seth's townhouse, that her romance crumbled down around her.

"I don't know how to say this nicely, so I'm going to give it to you straight," Chandra said. "The townhouse is in two names. Not just Seth Utsch. Seth and Judy Utsch."

Linda cartwheeled through a range of emotions before seeing Seth that Thursday afternoon. She'd thrown whatever she could find, and put a dent in the wall with an apple spice Yankee candle. She screamed, and sobbed, and allowed her heart to break. She was now the one thing she'd sworn she'd never become: the other woman. When he finally arrived that night, she was spent, and just shook her head.

"Why?" she asked, and he just shrugged.

"You wouldn't have slept with me otherwise," he said. Seth leaned in, gave her a peck on the cheek, spun around and walked out the door, leaving her stunned and shaken.

She hadn't heard either from or of him for three years when she and Cathy ran into him at the mall. They'd been shopping for heels at Payless, and there he was, buying

Proactiv from the kiosk right outside the store. She walked right past him, but turned when she heard someone call her name. She didn't quite recognize him at first, but once realization dawned, her heart lodged in her throat. Here was Seth, looking as gorgeous as ever, flashing those dimples and making her forget the months of sobbing into her pillow and wondering what was *wrong* with her that she could've been suckered in so easily. She introduced him to Cathy in a shaky voice, and after a few short pleasantries, she grabbed Cathy's arm and bolted. The pain was still there. It was duller, like an old scab itching to be picked at again, but it was an urge she didn't dare allow herself to satisfy.

Seth called the next day. He begged her to let him come over and apologize for all the hurt he'd caused her. She relented, and he showed up with Chinese takeout and a bottle of expensive wine. It was over this dinner that she found out he'd lied about his age, and the Air Force. "I don't know why I did it," he said, shaking his head regretfully. "I think I was trying to impress you."

Seth went on to tell her how Judy had left him for a plumber. The joke had been on Judy, though. Since she came from money, and she and Seth had been married long enough, she'd ended up having to pay him a nice chunk of change in the settlement. In retaliation, Judy refused to let him see his son. And was that a tear he managed to squeeze out as he talked about his child?

He charmed Linda all over again, and she was particularly flattered that he didn't try to sleep with her, instead insisting that he wanted to regain her trust through a tentative friendship. Like a dope, she'd believed him.

It was only a week later that he asked her how she'd feel if he asked Cathy out. Even though he'd only talked to her for that one minute in the mall, he felt they'd really connected. It suddenly became clear to Linda. Seth didn't respect her—he never had. He'd sucked up to her and apologized over kung pao just to gain an "in" with Cathy. She grew furious all over again, at him for being such a self-centered con man, and at herself for falling for it a second time. She paced all night, ranting and wailing, ready to kill him. And then the fog in her mind cleared, and she knew what she could do.

Exactly what he wanted.

The next day, she called him back with Cathy's number. She'd contacted Cathy first, to make sure it was okay. Her friend was enthusiastic, but would only date Seth "if it wouldn't be too uncomfortable for you, of course," and Linda assured her it would be fine. She was a big girl. She could handle it.

Seth and Cathy dated for six weeks before announcing their engagement. They asked Linda to be a bridesmaid at the wedding, which she'd found heartless and appalling, but she sucked it up and wore the tacky orange cocktail dress Cathy picked out. They'd been married for only a year when Seth suddenly took ill, complaining of stomach pains over the course of the week leading up to his death. The coroner's report had yet to come in, but Cathy was already tearfully telling people it must have been a perforated ulcer.

***

Linda let her manicured hand rest on the lapel of Seth's suit for the briefest of moments. Seth was Cathy's fourth husband. The first had accidentally dropped a radio into the tub he was soaking in; the second had also succumbed to a perforated ulcer. Husband number three fell off a cliff while he and Cathy were hiking through the Appalachians. Linda and Cathy met shortly after that, when Cathy moved to Connecticut to "leave all that bad juju behind."

Linda smiled down at Seth in his coffin and patted his collar. She hadn't known for *sure* if Cathy was actually responsible for her first three husbands' deaths.

But she'd hoped.

NOBODY EVER LISTENS TO EDDIE

Eddie is pouring his first cup of coffee when the bad feeling hits him. *Something terrible is going to happen today*, he thinks, and the despair is so overwhelming the mug in his hand shakes, splashing the counter. He drops his cup and doubles over, dazed.

Something horrible is coming.

It is not the first time Eddie Reynolds has gotten a sour sense of things. But it is certainly the strongest. He pushes himself upright again with trembling hands, and turns to the phone on the wall. Whom should he call first? His sister? His wife? Both have been scornful of his "premonitions" in the past, but this one, this dark cloud that has suddenly sunk icy black tentacles into his very soul, cannot be ignored. He won't be able to think of anything else until he knows his sister and wife are okay. Norma will probably not even take his call, but maybe if he talks to his sister first, can convince *her* . . .

Bev first, then.

Eddie dials Bev's number, Trinity-0529, and wonders what he's going to say.

***

Eddie was only five the first time he got a bad feeling. He was watching Beverly ride her bike without training wheels, wobbling down the sidewalk in front of their house, when a sharp pain came out of nowhere and stabbed its way up his elbow. He was so startled he shouted "Oh! Oooh!" which, of course, distracted his sister. She turned to look at what had attacked her brother, swerved off the sidewalk, hit a large rock, and flew over the handlebars. Bev sat in the road, screeching, cradling her elbow, her bent bicycle forgotten in the street. Eddie looked at his own arm, the one he'd been rubbing to make the throbbing stop, then blinked at his sister. The connection was as undeniable as their matching pain. Somehow he'd known this was going to happen. Had *sensed* it.

Eddie tried to tell his mother about the premonition of disaster, but Mom was too busy attending to his sobbing sister to listen. Later, when Bev was sitting on an orange couch in the ER, waiting for someone to plaster-cast her sprained elbow, he tried telling her. Bev scowled at him. "Stop it, Eddie. If you want attention, go sprain *your* arm and see how it feels." She sniffled.

After a while, Eddie had forgotten about the sympathy pains he'd gotten right before Bev's accident, but his bad feelings kept popping up, refusing to be disregarded.

When he was eight, he woke one morning knowing— just *knowing*—that he shouldn't go to church that day. But his parents insisted, ignoring his protests and making him wash behind his ears before putting on his Sunday best. And hadn't he thrown up right when he was about to receive communion? Sprayed Father Ross's pristine white robes with the remnants of that morning's eggs and orange juice? Eddie had *known*. But nobody had listened.

And there was that time with Toady. He'd found a toad, crouched right near the storm drain in the street, after it had rained for four days straight. Eddie was elated to find a new pet. But . . . there was something ominous about this toad. The skin on Eddie's arm prickled as he reached for the amphibian, making him hesitate.

It's just a toad, he argued with himself. *You can put him in a shoebox and call him Toady.* But he could sense something else. It felt—it felt like—"Death," Eddie whispered, and the word tasted rancid in his mouth.

The toad blinked at him indifferently. Eddie shook off his nervousness—he *knew* he was being ridiculous. He carefully scooped the creature up in his hands, cradling it to his chest. The toad immediately whizzed all over Eddie.

"Gross!" Eddie yelped, and instinctively flicked his hand to shake away the pee. Toady went flying, landing with a distinct *splat*. He kicked his little froggy legs once, then promptly died.

Eddie looked at the dead amphibian and burst into tears. Why had he picked the toad up at all? He should've just left him alone. But no, despite his bad feeling, Eddie had gone ahead and grabbed the toad anyway. He replayed the scene over and over in his head on his walk home. When he found his sister in the living room, listening to *The Shadow* on the radio, he announced to her that he was psychic. Bev listened to his tale and scoffed.

"Jeez, don't flip your wig! The toad just surprised you is all." She laughed and shooed him away.

***

Bev's mockery of his psychic abilities led Eddie to start keeping quiet about his funny feelings. When Eddie was about thirteen, his father came home with a new car. It was a shiny black DeSoto Airflow, all polished and clean with the faint aroma of new rubber. The stench of preordained calamity seemed to seep from every nut and bolt. Eddie's stomach lurched at the sight of it. But he said nothing, fearful of his sister's taunts.

"Come on out, boy, and we'll take it for a test drive," his father boomed, and Eddie couldn't say no. His father was a big guy, and very clear about how a young man should act, which was to follow his father's orders without question at all times, unless said young man wanted a meaty open-palmed swat upside the head. Eddie reluctantly climbed into the passenger seat and let his father take them for a spin down the block. He kept a white-knuckled grip on the door handle, not sure what might be coming—the car could catch on fire, Eddie mused, or the wheels could roll right off the base—but he knew from the telltale acid bubbling up in his throat that *something* was bound to happen. They made it down the street, past the big climbing tree on the corner, and came around full circle, all without incident. It wasn't until they pulled back into the driveway of their house that Eddie heard the crunch.

As soon as the Airflow stopped rolling, Eddie leapt from the car. He circled the black behemoth, looking for something—a fallen piece of airplane, a dead body under the wheels, *anything* to explain the hideous crunch he had heard. He found the source at the front of the car. There, crushed into the narrow, leering grill of the DeSoto, was the crumpled body of what originally was probably an impressive black bird.

"Whatcha got there, son?" Eddie's father chuckled. Eddie turned to his father, a limp, bloody feather pinched between two fingers.

"Dad . . . your new car ate a crow," he said.

"That's some impressive horsepower, by golly!" his father roared, clapping Eddie on the back hard enough that the tacky feather fluttered to the ground. "Let's go see what your mother's cooking up for dinner, shall we?"

Eddie thought more about the car after supper. His uneasiness over the new monstrosity parked out front hadn't let up any, even after he'd hosed the bird bits off the grille. There was something *wrong* about that car. He just didn't know what.

The answer came a year later, when his father was driving the Airflow home from his job as a presser at the Acme Brick Company in Fort Worth. The phone rang while Eddie's mother was frosting a chocolate Bundt cake.

"What? Wait, what happened, dear?" Eddie's ears perked up at his father's shouting on the other end of the line, loud enough for Eddie to hear at the kitchen table.

"The goddamned engine fell out of the car. Out! Of! The! Car!" his father bellowed.

That's what Eddie had been waiting for.

He'd just known something bad was going to happen with that DeSoto.

***

Bev picks up the phone after four rings. "Hello?" She sounds distracted.

"Hey, big sister," Eddie says, hoping his voice sounds natural. "How you been?"

"Eddie? It's nine o'clock in the morning. Why aren't you at work?" Since their parents died, Bev has become the resident fussbudget and worrywart. Eddie can understand why she's concerned that he's home at this hour.

"Took the day off. Heading into the city in a bit," Eddie says, and Bev murmurs understanding. "You going?"

"You know I can't. I still have to clean the house for Thanksgiving, and besides, Victor has the car. What's new with you? Any word from Norma? She coming home any time soon?"

Norma is Eddie's wife, and she left him three months ago to move back in with her mother.

"No, no word," Eddie mumbles.

"So what's up? It's not like you to call on a weekday like this unless—oh, no. Please tell me you're not calling for *that*."

But he is. "It's just—it's the worst feeling I've ever had, Bev. Just the most horrible one yet."

"Oh, Eddie," Bev starts.

"Honestly, it's never been this bad. Something awful is going to happen today, I know it. Do you think I wanted to call you and have you get mad at me like this? But—just be careful today, okay? I'm really worried that someone's going to get hurt real bad. Maybe even *die*." He chokes on this last word, afraid that if he says it out loud, he'll speak it into being.

"Damn it, Eddie, you've got to stop doing this! You're

practically neurotic. I'm so tired of hearing about your stupid hunches. Nothing bad is gonna happen. You need to stop worrying about every possible terrible thing that might be lurking around the corner, and go live your life!"

"That's not fair," he says impatiently. "How about when Norma called me at work in the middle of the day when Dad died? I *knew* she was calling with bad news."

"You knew that your wife, who never called you during the day unless it was an emergency, was calling with an emergency? Come on, now. Do you hear yourself?"

"Well, I knew Norma was going to leave, didn't I? I was right on the money about that one," Eddie snaps defensively.

"Of course Norma left you—hell, *I* could've told you that was coming down the pike. She can't stand your ridiculous premonitions either. You've got to stop this, Eddie, before you lose everyone in your life who's important to you. Please," Bev adds, her tone turning to a gentle entreaty. "I love you. Get help. There's a good doctor in Fort Worth you can talk to. Victor met him at a conference in Dallas just last month—"

"Bev! Stop it. I'm serious this time. And my feelings have never been wrong before."

Bev snorts. "No, no, that's not quite it. I think you meant to say your feelings have never been *right* before."

"That's not fair! How about the time I told you not to go out with Buck Fredericks, and you did anyway? And he ditched you at the Winter Wonderland dance to go make out with Edna Lutz?"

"Buck Fredericks was a fathead, and Edna Lutz was a tramp. Still is," Bev adds with a chuckle. "I heard she's waitressing at the Carousel Club, and you know no good God-fearing Christian would dare set foot in that mobbed-up dive. Serves her right. But seriously, Eddie, anyone could've predicted that date was gonna end badly. Mom begged me not to go out with Buck. Even I didn't want to go, but Martha needed someone to pair up with Buck so she could go out with his friend Frankie."

"What about the time you fell off your bike? Or when my toad died?" Eddie knows he's grasping at straws—Bev has always had a rational explanation for his mystical predictions—but he can't stop himself. "I *knew*—"

"There you go with your three favorite words again: 'I knew it.' Funny how you never tell anyone what's about to happen before it actually happens, Eddie. Do you hear yourself? If you go around predicting that bad things are gonna happen, sooner or later, you'll be right. I broke a nail this morning when I was scrubbing the breakfast plates. Then I accidentally wet my pants a little when I sneezed. I'm surprised you didn't call emergency services before those awful calamities befell me."

Eddie pauses for a moment. Could the broken nail be what he's sensing? No, that's—

"Oh for God's sake. Talk to a doctor. I think you might be certifiably crazy," Bev says. "Now, if you'll excuse me, I have to start washing the walls before we have all those people here next week. And Eddie? Do yourself a favor. Don't call Norma about this. If you want to win her back, for the love of God, stop pestering her with your stupid 'bad feelings.'"

Bev hangs up, and Eddie listens to the drone of the dial tone. Maybe his sister is right. After all, the 1934 DeSoto

Airflow was notorious for dropping its engine in the middle of the road; his father's woes hadn't been anything special ... but no. His fists clench as the sense of approaching disaster crawls over his skin again like a funeral shroud. He simply must call Norma. To warn her.

***

"Hey, pumpkin," Eddie says nervously when Norma answers the phone. "I was just thinking about you."

"That's sweet," Norma says, in her whispery lilt, and Eddie's heart drums out an off beat when he hears her. God, he misses her breathless, breezy voice around the house.

"How've you been?" he asks, suddenly shy. "How's your mom?"

"Fine," Norma says meekly. "Mom's not feeling too good today. We were hoping to head into the city, you know, but now I'm not sure ..."

"I'm going there myself," Eddie cuts in. "Maybe we ... I could meet you?"

Norma sighs. "I don't know if that's a good idea."

"But I miss you so much," he confesses.

"I miss you too," Norma echoes, and Eddie's spirits soar, just for a second, until she adds "but unless things change, I can't be with you. Not any more."

It's the children issue, Eddie knows. Norma wants them, and Eddie does too, or so he'd thought. But when they started really trying to make it happen, Eddie had been seized with such terror, such certainty that having kids would be a horrible mistake ... well, he hadn't been able to finish the job in the bedroom, so to speak. Sometimes, when he would listen to Norma cry herself to sleep, he'd tell himself he was being ridiculous—every guy worried about becoming a father, it was natural, and had nothing to do with his frightening intuition—but then he'd think of his own dad, and knew deep down that Big Ed had never worried, not one minute, about being a good father. No, this was something worse. If Eddie and Norma had kids, something terrible would happen. Eddie can just feel it. He moans, and within that moan lives the weight of his sorrows, the bleakness of his life, his worries; his very existence.

"Eddie? Do you understand?" Norma asks softly. Her voice, too, is heavy with regret.

"I know. It's just—how can we start a family when something awful might happen? How can we knowingly do that to our children?"

"Eddie." The whisper and light are gone from her voice. Her tone is cold steel. "Bad things happen to everyone. Good things happen, too. I won't live my life with a man who's too preoccupied with all the ways things might go wrong that he can't see the joy and delight in all the wonderful things going on around him, every day. I can't live like that, and I hate that you choose to."

Eddie's shoulders slump. He feels it the moment it happens: a sense of relief, of giving up. *I can't control the future. Whatever's gonna happen is just gonna happen. Norma's right. I hate living like this. And I'm driving her away.*

He can't have that.

He opens his mouth, hesitates, and breathes deeply. "I understand what you're saying, Norma. I do. And you're right. I don't want to live this way, always starting a new project or job or day with a bad feeling. I hate that I do that. I—what if I—I can promise to try, okay? Will you at least give me a little time to try?"

Norma responds with the best sound Eddie has heard in a long time: her melodic laugh, a sweet giggle that makes Eddie laugh, too.

"Really? Do you mean it?"

"Listen, I'm planning on leaving the house in about twenty minutes. Why don't I swing by, pick you up, and we can head into the city together? Then you can decide for yourself if I mean it or not."

"Okay. Yes. I'd love to!"

***

Eddie's practically dancing as he hangs up the phone and goes upstairs to put on his cleanest suit. His smile wavers for a moment when he realizes his shoes desperately need a good polishing. The cold tentacles of impending doom start to slither up his skin again, but he thinks of Norma's pretty little laugh and shakes away the dread before it can take hold. *Who's going to be looking at my feet, anyway?* he thinks, and pulls his dress shoes on, smudges and all.

Eddie fishes his best hat out of the closet and pops it on his head. He looks in the mirror and tilts the brim a little, feeling like Bogie, off to pick up his best girl, Lauren Bacall. He steps outside. The sun is shining. Eddie whistles as he walks to his car.

It's a beautiful day. Eddie's going to pick up his gorgeous wife and drive her to Dallas. Maybe they can even have a picnic in Dealey Plaza. President Kennedy is in town, and for the first time in Eddie's fearful life, he feels optimistic. *Today*, he tells himself, *will be a good day.*

THE STORIES BEHIND THE STORIES

SECRET THINGS was a fun little tale I penned for a magazine contest. I didn't win, but I enjoyed the story so much I thought it deserved face time here.

GOOD NIGHT, FRANCINE is largely based on a member of my family. We don't associate with him at all, but Francine is what I imagine he's like, except she's a little tamer.

TIME TO LET GO's main character, Ben, is based on a Ben I knew in college. The ladies loved him, but sadly, he died much too young. This story is a little homage to his memory.

CLIFFHANGER came about when I was sitting in an employment law conference, bored out of my mind. The two lawyers hosting the presentation, Victor and Holly, had a much more interesting day in the story I scribbled out in an effort to stay awake during the OSHA portion of the presentation.

JOSEPHINE was inspired by a conversation I had with a former coworker about her first love. She was in her fifties, and still not over this guy who had never really paid much attention to her. I thought it was sad. Imagine waiting your whole life for someone who's just not that into you?

LOVE STINKS is my commentary on how people do some pretty stupid things for love. My advice: if your significant other is a zombie, it's time to break up.

TRAPPED was written during the winter of 2011, when I was on crutches for four months after cracking my kneecap during a misguided ice skating adventure. It was one of the worst winters we'd ever had in Connecticut. I was definitely stir crazy, which manifested into this story.

MAX ELLIOTT, EXTERMINATOR: I love Max. He's a cross between my Dad and actor Sam Elliott, and he's had cameos in a few of my short stories. He's a great character; I just haven't been able to do much with him. Give him time; he'll star in a zombie apocalypse novel sooner or later.

PEOPLE PERSON was the second short story I ever sold (for something like ¼ cent per word), and the first to make it to print. I lived on a small island for ten years, and I wanted to convey how lonely it can be, even in a close-knit community. Cobb is a conglomerate of several people I knew on the island. And no, I didn't kill anyone while I lived out there.

MOTHER'S DAY was written in response to a specific call for submissions. I tried so hard to make Ella sound nothing like my mother, and Mama nothing like my grandmother, but re-reading it, I can see just about every woman in my life in there (including my mother, aunts, sister, and my mother's best friend). I like to think my late grandmother would find this story a hoot.

DENNY'S DILEMMA: My senior year of high school, something like eight people I knew died in different and sometimes odd ways. Talk about teenage angst! As I got older, I thought *who am I to question why it happened? Maybe their lives would've been terrible.* It's that kind of fun question that inspires stories like this one.

WOMAN SCORNED is a fanciful little tale in which I kill off one of my ex-boyfriends. I'd *almost* forgiven him for being a rotten, conniving liar. Writing this story helped. He's still alive and well, by the way. Don't date him.

NOBODY EVER LISTENS TO EDDIE was inspired by two things: one, my mother insists that she gets "feelings," and swears they're always right. (Most notably, in 1991, she once called me at college because she had a "feeling" I was sad. To her credit, I was.) The other is a frustrating thing I run into all the time: I have a pretty remarkable memory for conversations. However, most people don't, and when

I parrot back what someone said to me in June 2013, they'll insist I either made it up or that they never said it. Believe me, I feel Eddie's pain.

ACKNOWLEDGMENTS

What you hold in your hands is not the first iteration of *Secret Things*. When it was published in 2013, I knew the *value* of an editor, but was too inexperienced to recognize a good one from a bad one. As a result, several errors slipped past the red pen. In the time since, I wound up embarking on my second career, this time as a copyeditor. When I picked up *Secret Things* one afternoon and flipped through it, I was mortified. And immediately called and editor, Rob Smales. So thank you, Rob, for fixing this mess, and for not making fun of me.

Thank you to my family for letting me observe your most private experiences and character traits and subsequently exploit them for a good story.

Many thanks to my fellow writers for their feedback: Catherine Grant, Jan Kozlowski, and Kristi Petersen Schoonover. You ladies of horror rock!

ABOUT THE AUTHOR

Stacey Longo is the author of *Ordinary Boy*, nominated for a Pushcart Prize in 2016. Her novella "Brando and Bad Choices" was featured in *Triplicity: The Terror Project, Volume 1*. She has also penned two books designed to help explain multiple sclerosis to children (*My Mom Has MS* and *My Mom, MS, and a Sixth-Grade Mess*) in honor of her friend Renee and to help raise money for the National MS Society.

Longo's stories have appeared in numerous anthologies and magazines, including *Shroud*, *Shock Totem*, and the *Litchfield Literary Review*. She is a past Hiram Award winner, and was a featured author on the 2014 Connecticut Authors Trail. A former humor columnist for the *Block Island Times*, she maintains a weekly humor blog at www.staceylongo.com.